CAT SOCIETY

CAT
SOCIETY

Ray Sadri

The Book Guild Ltd

First published in Great Britain in 2023 by
The Book Guild Ltd
Unit E2 Airfield Business Park,
Harrison Road, Market Harborough,
Leicestershire. LE16 7UL
Tel: 0116 2792299
www.bookguild.co.uk
Email: info@bookguild.co.uk
Twitter: @bookguild

This work is entirely fictitious and bears no resemblance to any persons living or dead.

Typeset in 11pt Minion Pro

ISBN 978 1915853 226

British Library Cataloguing in Publication Data.
A catalogue record for this book is available from the British Library.

Dedicated to Mads, Fee, and every cat around the world. We know you're observing and taking notes…

ACT ONE

MIDNIGHT IN WHITEHALL

Douglas peered through the bins at the scraggly she-cat.

'Uh, evening, miss, could I bother you for a moment?' he said, making sure his tail was pointing upwards.

She was licking the remnants of mushed tuna off her paw.

'Depends. What can I do for you?'

The tuna smelt like it had gone off. The stink got up his nostrils.

'My name is Douglas Schnitty —'

'Ah, you have a surname, you must be a politician?'

'Yes, I have the honour of representing you as your Member of Parliament. It's a pleasure to meet you.'

She huffed. 'Oh God, don't even bother.'

'I beg for just two minutes of your time. I've come to visit you because I would really like your, uh, views. They are important.'

She froze next to her makeshift fire; her pretty, green eyes glowing. He looked around and saw dozens of rough sleepers lying next to the bins. There were hardly any tomcats about, the vast majority seemed to be she-cats. The bins were arranged close together in a higgledy-piggledy fashion.

A pair of skinny kittens were loitering, marking a magpie. They kept their eyes on the long-tailed fellow, as he chattered and skipped about, oblivious to the danger he was in. This was the third slum Douglas had seen in Westminster this week, they were cropping up fast.

'Look, I know it's difficult right now,' he continued. 'We're trying to make things better —'

'Surprised to see you here if I'm honest. The election's been and gone, you can relax.'

'Yes, but I'm trying to figure out how things have got like this. Can I ask what your story is? Why have you ended up here?'

'Ran my own business for two years, I did. In the fashion industry. Stitching designer collars for the classy she-cats — you know, the catesses. Like this one.' She lowered her head and held out a soft brown leather collar.

'Oh, wow, that's beautiful.' Douglas ran his paw along the embroidered fish pattern. 'So, what went wrong?'

'Well, orders pretty much dropped overnight. Nobody had the money to spend on luxury goods anymore. Lost the premises, had to sack my staff, and went under just before the election.'

'I'm really sorry, uh…'

'Mandy.' The pointy-eared Balinese cat started to untangle her matted hair with her teeth. She was an attractive she-cat. 'Lost my home too. Couldn't afford the rent and the landlord didn't waste any time in kicking me out. Tried for social housing but all the tree estates are chocka. Ended up out here in the bins.'

'I am so sorry, Mandy. I will see to it that the Prime

Minister hears your story, loud and clear.' And he meant it, he would request a meeting first thing in the morning. Something needed to be done.

'I've been on the social housing waiting list for six weeks. I'm praying that a cabin in one of the trees will free up any day now, just down the way. Not ideal, but at least they're better than this.'

'Mandy, let me look into that for you. May I ask, did you vote in the last election?'

She started scratching viciously at her ear. 'Course I did. Couldn't wait to see the back of the Cats Collective. They taxed me to the hilt and ran the economy into the ground. They screwed us lot who were working hard and making an honest living. Are you one of them?'

'No, no. I am your local Freedom Cat MP, part of Marjorie Wilson's government.'

'Well, I voted for you. But you lot need to help us fast. We're literally dying out here. Tell CatSaver queen to sort it. No time to snooze.'

'Uh, CatSaver queen?'

'Yeah, I think she's alright, but in the fashion business, we call her "CatSaver queen" cos that's clearly where she buys her tacky collars from.'

'Really? I thought she's quite fashionable for a Prime Minister.'

'You've got to be kidding me.' Mandy winced. 'Those glittery collars and gaudy bows are horrible. Can't believe the Prime Minister would shop at CatSaver.'

There was smoke rising behind her. It looked like a cat high on nip was setting a bin alight. Douglas spotted the kittens; the little terrors had succeeded in nabbing their prey. They were tucking into their magpie special.

'You, however,' she continued, 'you're way too good looking to be an MP.'

Douglas looked into her emerald-like eyes and treated her to one of his coy smiles. 'That's, uh, very kind of you.'

'And you have a cute smile. I always think smiling doesn't suit us cats, we never really mastered it. But you're a natural.'

He was getting late for his nightly swim. 'Thanks, Mandy. Look, I must get going. And, uh, take this bandage for your ear. Keep it clean, it's looking infected.'

'Thank you, Mr Schnitty. Tell the PM to help us, yeah? Or the riots and looting will get far worse.'

*

Around the corner, on the fifth floor of the Ministry of Defence building in Whitehall, Hector made a phone call. He had got through half a bottle of moonshot — beet juice infused with cat nip, topped with a splash of spring water — and he felt sick. This bottle had cost well over 100 British Mews, and it sure as hell was some of the strongest out there. It had a whopping 55 per cent cat nip content, twice as much as the normal stuff, and it was British grown. He approved of that. He also approved of the spring water being sourced from the Highlands.

'To whom am I speaking?' Hector slurred. Angus the journalist politely informed him that it was *he*, *Hector*, who had in fact made the call in the first place.

'Ah, very well. Hector Perp Pahpousson here.'

The journalist patiently informed him that he was aware of the caller's identity.

'Yahh, I love *The Meowington Times,* you know. I feel I can speak freely with your… your readers. We are aligned, spiritually, socio-economically… I wouldn't dream of talking to the boohahs at the *Daily Mog.* Now then, we are in quite the conundrum, aren't we?'

'Are we?' came the response.

'Hang on a moment.' He stumbled across to his giant gold-plated cream fountain. He was rather chuffed with it. He was glad he had insisted for it to be installed. Bang in the centre of his office. On his first day in the job. Even if it did rile the jobsworth of the building manager upstairs who kept quoting some outdated building regulation at him. What a bore.

He stuck his large, round face under the grand six-foot tall structure. *Shlop, shlop, shlop.* He caught the thick luscious double cream on his tongue, as it flowed down the five rotating tiers. He closed his eyes, lapping up the velvety liquid as it splattered all over his luxurious long black hair. Cream was definitely a proven hangover remedy. A good slug of it had gathered in the bucket underneath and he was looking forward to devouring it for breakfast later.

'Prrr-au! I'm back,' said Hector. He half closed his twitchy eyes. 'As I was saying, we are in a dire situation. I have received reliable intelligence that those Russian Blue and Siberian Cat armies have put their domestic differences to one side. They are grouping at their respective borders, they are taking up arms, and they have us very much in their sights.'

The new Defence Secretary looked round at the national flag proudly draped on the wall behind his desk. Known as the 'eyes and claws', it featured a pair of bright yellow cat eyes and ten claws, symbolising an offer of protection to the nation. He loved doing media interviews sitting in front of it, with the special eyes looking down on him.

'We need more planes and gunboats at once, show them we are not to be messed with,' declared the black Chinchilla, his chubby face covered in cream. 'We must rule the air and the waves once again, but we need the proper bloody funding for that to happen. The Prime Minister, you know, er, Marjorie, she needs to toughen up. Hopefully, she will start to listen. I am a military cat, after all.'

He heard some boring question about how much funding would be needed. He sniffed on the latest first-class delivery sent to him by the *Chew Chew Club*. Inside was his latest nip leaf order — the finest catnip and ground cashew nut delicately rolled in bloodleaf, and bound together with fishpaste. He loved this variety. Moonshot was his friend, but this stuff never failed to send him to the stars. And chewing nip leaf was definitely good for his teeth, no matter what those pesky veterinarians said.

'She also needs to fund my wall idea, have I mentioned that?' shrieked Hector, feeling a sudden burst of energy. 'Hordes of moggies from Malta and the Greek Islands are attempting to cross Europe and settle here for a better life. Truth is we have run out of space, we do not have the resources. My big, beautiful wall will stop them. Keep the strays out.'

'How much are we talking?' asked the journalist.

Hector looked around in admiration. He had the biggest office out of all his Cabinet colleagues, he had visited them to make sure, and damn right too. He scanned the walls, every inch plastered with framed pictures of himself – giving speeches to awestruck Members of the House, posing with celebrities and heads of state, close-ups of him chewing nip leaf contemplatively, and even napping in various cities around the country.

'What's that?' said Hector. 'Hello, hi? How much will it cost, you ask? Well, look, I am confident that we can build a tall enough border wall for 14 million British Mews.'

He frowned. 'What? Ah, yes, it may sound like a lot right now, but remember that our currency will eventually bounce back. The British Mew is already rising against the Cat Dollar. And anyway, we absolutely mustn't put a price on our security.'

He licked at a stubborn splodge of cream on his fur. 'What do you mean we are an island? So?'

He chewed on his nip leaf noisily. 'I shouldn't even be talking to you lot at *The Meowington Times*, you know. Little miss Prime Minister, that Marjorie Wilson, has banned me from giving press interviews. But I need your fine readers on side, it's the only way she'll listen and give us the dosh that we so badly need for our security. Hello, hi?'

Thwack! Hector whacked the phone on his desk. 'Ah, yes, there you are. As I was saying we need moolah for our military, and I know just how to find it. Now then, do you know how many trees there are just in our Capital? Let me tell you, eight million.'

He paused for reaction. 'Now, we may have taken them over for our own housing needs, driven the squirrels out of them, and rightly so! But the fact is, most of the trees along the embankment and in our glorious parks are standing empty due to their prime positioning. They're listed, you know, out of bounds. They can't be occupied.'

He plonked himself down and rolled over onto his back. The journalist began asking something about easing the strict tree protection regulations. Hector cut him off. 'Let's encourage the Dragon Lis and the Persians to sponsor these beauties. They are loaded; we could easily command in the region of half a million British Mews per tree if we market this right. That would fill our military coffers and any surplus can go towards the border wall. Imagine, my friend, imagine…'

Hector began to snore mid-sentence.

MAKING THINGS RIGHT

'Come on, keep going,' Douglas urged himself. He was swimming in the river under Putney Bridge, thrusting his legs, using all the strength he could muster. 'Push! A little more.' He was wheezing heavily, throat numb.

The bright orange sun was rising; the trees along the embankment were watching over him. *Must get to a mile, no ifs, no buts.* Douglas pushed and pushed until his body gave way. He could go on no longer.

He let out a long groan. *It shouldn't have ended this way. I could have done more. I should have done more.* He drifted along. The sun's beautiful orange glow reflected onto the water. He felt a cool sensation wash over his athletic body; it relaxed him. He was pulling himself back together, breath by breath.

That homeless she-cat he had met earlier popped into his head — Mandy. The one with the gorgeous green eyes. Running her own business, making designer collars — what an entrepreneur. He loved her story. And then losing everything and being thrown onto the scrap heap, pretty much overnight. *Tragic.*

He was pissed off with the Prime Minister. She'd been admirably quick in responding to his meeting request. He recollected the cold words of her email. *The Prime Minister regrets that she is unable to meet due to her busy schedule. However,* it had continued, *the Prime Minister has asked if you would be interested in joining her Emergency Money Saving Committee?*

The Committee was completely irrelevant to struggling cats like Mandy. Plus, the workload seemed immense, and he couldn't bear the thought of sitting in hours of dull meetings, listening to wonks talking to themselves in their bureaucratic speak, getting nowhere. And above all, he didn't agree with her planned cuts. They were way too extreme.

He thought of Mandy again. Despite everything, she still supported Marjorie Wilson. For now, anyway. Her worst criticism was about her collars being tacky. That was quite something. There were thousands like Mandy, forced to live in the bins because of the incompetence of the last government. The last thing the poor sods needed now was austerity.

He thought about his ex. The big moment in court was a few hours away; at least there would be some closure after months of pointless mediation, months of haggling, and months of bitterness. Whatever happened, he would finally be able to move on.

Back to the Prime Minister's stupid Money Saving Committee; it could be an easy way to try to get through to her, perhaps encourage her to show a bit of empathy. He could grit his teeth and accept the Committee position; he'd think about it some more. But for now, it was back to the swimming. He needed to improve his technique, and he needed to improve quickly.

He felt a sudden burst of pride and began purring. Proud that he'd turned up to swim every single night without fail. Up and down, between the bridges, nothing would stop him on his quest to reach a mile. He would never give up. It wasn't his choice. This would be the only way he could make things right after everything that happened. He would make damn sure he made things right.

THE VERDICT

Douglas felt as if his teeth were about to fall out as he lugged the giant Canada Goose into the court room. The panel of judges had better notice the fresh scent of the bird, hunted just this morning. There they were, the three of them staring at him intently. They were covered in their black silks. He lowered his head as he approached and plonked the hefty offering at their paws. That was a relief.

'Uh, Douglas Schnitty reporting to you, m'lords.' He noticed a hamper of fine meats to the side — poussin, pigeon, juicy cuts of mice. Shit, that would be from her, she'd only gone and outdone him. And there she was in the corner of his eye, he felt her glare on him, like a laser beam burning a hole through his ear. He had promised himself he wouldn't make eye contact but couldn't help himself. She looked like she'd been crying. She was wearing a holey t-shirt and odd socks. Funny that, she was the biggest snob he'd ever met, and she had always dressed immaculately in all their time together. They kept their eyes locked on each other.

'Attention!' said the judge in the middle. He tapped his paw three times on the table he was sitting on. 'The Court of the Cats has reached a decision in the case of Tamara versus Douglas Schnitty.'

Douglas closed his eyes. He tried to ignore his shaky tail.

'Please rise,' ordered the lead judge.

Douglas lurched onto to his clammy paws, looking straight ahead. It would be OK; the system was fair, he told himself. After all, she was the one who had left him, plus she came from good stock. She was far from going hungry, that was for sure.

The trio upfront seemed to be conferring, it looked as if they were debating some sort of last-minute technicality.

They would have taken into account the 500 British Mews he had to pay her every month since she had walked out, as she was still technically a mother. It was one of those loopy bits of law imported from the Global Cats Alliance.

'Douglas Schnitty,' said the judge.

'It will be fine,' muttered Douglas to himself.

'You will give your mansion to Tamara.'

Douglas kept his gaze fixed straight ahead. He was trying to focus on the words he'd just heard. Something about giving the mansion to Tamara. Mansion is Tamara's. Tamara gets mansion.

'Wait, what? How —' blurted out Douglas.

'Quiet!' shouted the judge on the left. His abnormally large fang was terrifying.

The mansion? He couldn't have heard right, he had bought the damn mansion himself, it was in his name. 'Uh, m'lord —'

'I said, quiet!' the one on the left hissed at him.

'Douglas Schnitty, you will sign over your mansion plus 50 per cent of your earnings every month to the mother of your kitten.'

'This must be some sort of mistake, m'lord. I will become homeless overnight. I have nowhere else to —'

'Final warning!' snarled the fanged one. 'You may be a politician, and you may have given yourself a surname and whatnot, but you are not above this court!'

The one in the middle continued. 'Mr Schnitty, you have 72 hours to vacate your home. The monthly payments from your wages will be effective immediately for a period of two years. I would strongly advise you not to miss any.'

Douglas shuddered. He was well and truly stuffed.

'You are in a fortunate position, Mr Schnitty, and you have options, thanks to your politician's salary. Even 50 per cent of your earnings is more than what many have in these testing times. It could have been a lot worse for you.'

Fuck! Fuck! Fuck! This was a disaster. He obviously wouldn't qualify for a cabin in the trees; he had nowhere else to go.

The judges rose, clamping the Canada goose and hamper in between their teeth. The quiet one on the right whispered something in Tamara's ear before slipping out. His ex looked over with pitiful eyes. Douglas hunched over. He felt sick.

OUR TREES
ARE FULL

Jitters leapt into his safe room. It was the biggest and airiest of the unruly maze of hiding spots he had constructed in his office on Horse Guards Road, and it was his favourite one to practice his lines from. The walls were padded, the acoustics were better, and he was well hidden from the outside world. He could screw up his lines and get in a muddle as much as he wanted from inside there, and nobody would ever know.

The grey, broad-chested cat checked CatKiss again. He had last checked seven minutes ago; you never know, perhaps there was a message from her. They had hit it off really well, she had laughed at his jokes and seemed keen to meet up, so why the silence all of a sudden? He looked up at the portrait of his ma that he had painted recently. It comforted him. He had found a note from her in his snack box, *Congrats on the promotion Jitsy, cream always rises to the top, proud of you. Love Ma x.* He folded it up carefully and placed it in his drawer.

Indeed, it was a promotion. Jitters peeked at his pile of papers. His to-do list had doubled in the last 24 hours. He noticed a memo from the Prime Minister's office. *For the urgent attention of Jitters Renshaw, Minister for Welfare and General Sums.* It went on to say that the next round of debt reduction policy ideas had to be submitted to the Emergency Money Saving Committee by the end of the week. It had her very own paw print at the bottom, next to her name. *The Rt. Hon. Marjorie Wilson.* He knew the Committee was important to her, close to her heart. He'd heard that she had specifically asked for him to join it after hearing about his innovative thinking around the "oversized cabin penalty" for those in the tree estates.

'We are b-b-being very g-g-generous and g-g-g-giving cats on benefits t-t-t-tree cabins to live in,' he announced to himself.

'But many are hogging tree c-c-cabins too big for their n-n-needs...'

His nose began twitching. '... meanwhile thousands of f-f-families are stuck on waiting l-l-lists.'

He imagined the captivated audience in front of him, hanging on every word. 'They-They-They must d-d-downsize...'

He paused mid-sentence. 'Or have their b-b-benefits c-c-cut.'

He pulled out his flask and supped nervously on some tepid water. It had been a long night. 'This common sense policy will h-h-h-help hundreds of th-th-thousands by f-f-freeing up the b-b-b-books and balancing the branches. Damn it.'

He took a deep breath. 'I mean it f-f-frees up the branches AND it will slash the housing b-b-b-bill in this country. It will b-b-balance the books. Yes.'

He scrolled on CatKiss again. Surely the single she-cats out there would snap up a government minister? And who knew what would be in store for his career if he impressed and made his mark in the prestigious Emergency Money Saving Committee? He liked the new Prime Minister, Marjorie Wilson, and he was one hundred percent behind her programme of cuts. They were necessary after thirteen years of the Cats Collective screwing things up.

Jitters leapt down nervously to 'La Vista', his viewing cubbyhole. He looked out of the large window overlooking St James's Park. The oasis of green usually calmed him. Helped him order his thoughts. Tonight, however, the chants of 'No more cuu-uuts, get the Freedom Cat tossers out!' seemed to be getting louder as the night went on. He didn't like it.

He was still shaken from his journey into the office. He had just about dodged the rioting and looting which usually flared up around this time. He had to pass the homeless lot who had moved into the bins downstairs. They had started to recognise him now; they had clocked that he was somehow connected to the government. They usually growled and nipped at him; today one of them went as far as to chase him into the building. *Scruffs.*

He was proud to be at the heart of a new government trying to fix things. He could not for the life of him understand the fierce resistance from the tremendous alliance of public sector workers – the vets, nurses, teachers, and so on. He would tell the Prime Minister to stand firm. And this "oversized cabin penalty" he was working up would help save millions.

'Our trees are f-f-full!' he shouted, getting carried away.

'Selfish behaviour will be p-p-punished!' He soaked up the standing ovation in his head.

'Jitters will f-f-fix it!' The cheering was deafening, it drowned out the protests outside.

'Balance the trees, f-f-f-fix the books! Damn it!'

That was enough for this hardworking minister, it was time for a well-earned snooze. He clambered onto his slide down into the chill room. Nobody would find him there, it was warm, and he was safe from the world. Still nothing on CatKiss. She'd better not have ghosted him.

LYING IN WAIT

Douglas was lying in wait outside the back entrance of Number Ten. He had his yellow-gold silk tie on. It matched the colour of his eyes perfectly, he thought. And it contrasted well with his rich black fur. Double knotted and hanging nicely, a centimetre above ground. These things were important. They showed he meant business.

The Prime Minister would be on her way back from her weekly PMQs. He felt on edge. It hadn't fully sunk in that he was about to become officially homeless. Perhaps he could stay with Jitters for a while.

For now, he had an urgent job to do. He would confront the PM, make her see sense. He would tell her about the thousands living in the bins, the suffering taking place under her watch. There was no way he was going to be fobbed off by one of her standard letters. *The Prime Minister regrets that she is unable to meet due to her busy schedule.* 'We'll see about that,' he growled under his breath.

He crouched down low and kept still; she'd probably leg it if she caught any whiff of him. He went over the maths of a leadership challenge once again in his head. Yes, it was perhaps a bit over the top. It would be bonkers so soon after the last election. There wouldn't be much of an appetite for it in the Party, and the country wouldn't thank him either. Quite frankly, it was the last thing he needed in his life of turmoil right now, but he did the maths anyway.

He was sure he could persuade 15 per cent of his Party to submit a letter of no confidence. And if she lost the vote, which was a big if in itself, he would definitely get the support to make it through to the final two. That Hector would probably throw his hat in the contest; the Defence Secretary would be a tough opponent to beat. This was madness. If only the Prime Minister would listen and do the right thing.

Douglas heard a rustling and flinched. 'Uh, hi, Prime Minister, didn't realise you were right here.'

'What can I do for you, Douglas?'

He forced his tail upwards. It was important to show that he'd come in the spirit of friendship. 'Uh, I would like you to reconsider my request, and I would like you to come and meet my slum constituents. Come and meet Mandy, she —'

'Douglas, the country is in a terrible state, and I am working all hours to fix it. I haven't got the time to make, er… well, impromptu visits.'

'I understand, but those in the slum have lost everything, Prime Minister. They need help urgently.'

'Well, once we get our spending under control —'

'I'm sorry to interrupt, Prime Minister, but the thousands like Mandy cannot wait for that. Can we work together on a plan to get some basic emergency assistance to them?'

'Impossible at the moment.'

'But there must be a way we can free up more trees and get building mass cabins for them? They don't cost much.'

'Oy, Douglas, move it,' snarled her burly press secretary.

'But —'

'Sorry, Douglas, I'm late for my meeting with, er... I mean, *wiv*, the *Daily Mog*,' said the Prime Minister.

'With, not viv,' said the press guy.

'Yes, but I am, er... well, sounding relatable.'

February 2008

Jitters opened his eyes. He squinted in the bright light and made out a familiar shadow. 'Jitsy, darling! Oh, thank God you're awake. The chief vet says you're going to be OK.'

'Ma? What h-h-happened? Where a-a-am I?'

The kitten's eyes gave way again and he remembered feeling the cold, icy pavement on the side of his face. He remembered his soaking wet fur and how he could not feel his ears. He had kept going back home, kept scratching on the door, but it was locked.

'Why won't you l-l-let me in, p-p-pa?' He saw the curtain shuffle. There was silence. 'It's f-f-freezing, pa, p-p-please let me in. I'm sorry for making you a-a-angry, pa.'

He had been scrounging for food and supping on the snow for three days. His father had locked him out before, but these freezing weather conditions were the worst yet. He felt numb, he couldn't even feel himself urinating.

'Please, pa. I'm only f-f-five months old. I-I-I can't feel my tail. I'm s-s-scared, pa.'

Young Jitters came back round to the bright light, to the shiny white walls of the hospital, and to his ma's soothing voice. 'I am so sorry, my Jitsy, you had passed out by the time I found you. I promise I will never let him do that to you again. I will make sure you never have to fend for yourself like that ever again.'

*

Almost seven years to the day from his near-death experience, a plumper Jitters was first in line at the Commons Cafeteria. He stared as moggies in chef hats were causing mayhem, darting around the kitchen clumsily with their sharp knives, chopping pigeon and mice for their gourmet pies. At least fifty per cent of their output seemed to be going missing. 'Oy, you're on your last warning,' growled the head chef, 'stop gobbling up the bloomin' produce.'

Jitters was looking forward to sinking his teeth into a cream cheese and salmon bagel. His ma would have normally dished him up some scrambled eggs, but she had been poorly all night and he had persuaded her to rest. He grabbed himself two portions, after all he was ravenous, and he began to scurry back to his office.

'Jitters, old chap! Wait up, sir,' came a whisper behind him. 'Heartfelt felicitations on the gig, you'll be a top-class Minister for Welfare and General Sums. Just superb!'

'Th-Th-Thank you, Hector, and you t-t-too,' said Jitters, speeding up. He had important work to be getting on with, and he wasn't about to let his bagels go cold.

Hector stuck behind him. 'Say, Jitters, what do you make of the conundrum out there? I mean, the looting is out of control. Will we have to U-turn on this messy business of the Prime Minister's cuts?'

'It h-h-has to be d-d-done, I s-s-support it.'

'Well, of course you do, you are part of her special committee, I hear, and again, my heartfelt congratulations on that, sir! But she's had to order the courts to sit day and night to deal with the looters. It's getting —'

'Again, needs t-t-t-to be done. I know victims of abuse, poor f-f-families, that c-c-could not even g-g-get c-c-counselling or help from social s-s-services because the state had run out of m-m-money under the Cats C-C-Collective.'

Hector chewed on some nip leaf with a distracted look on his face. 'Of course, old chap, that's very sad. And do you know, the now chummy Siberian Cat and Russian Blue armies are hatching something together? It's a shame our military is cut to the bone, thanks to the flipping Collective idiots.'

'The-The-The only way things will improve is if we get the public f-f-finances under c-c-control. L-L-Look at what happened t-t-to the hoomans many decades ago. We must l-l-learn from them. Sh-Sh-She has to stand firm.'

'Absolutely correct, Jitters. This shambles is all the opposition's fault, and we need to keep an eye on them. If we're not careful, that Kranken and his band of crusties will… Well, they cannot —'

'Y-Y-Yes, they a-a-absolutely cannot be trusted with the p-p-public finances!'

'Yahhp, correct again, sir.' Hector paused, leaned in, and lowered his voice. 'The trouble is we have a spineless leader. I fear she may not last much longer, and let me tell you, your talents are being wasted under her. It is a tragedy.'

'W-W-Wasted?'

'Let's keep close, you and me, sir!'

Jitters could smell the moonshot on the Defence Secretary's breath. 'C-C-Close? How do you m-m-m —'

Before he could finish, Hector had wandered off. It looked as if he was about to retch.

NEW DAY, NEW SLUM

Douglas crouched on his hind legs observing. A middle-aged couple were having a barney by the bins. These slum cats didn't have mates like Jitters and Hector to put them up in their mansions, they needed help.

'When you gonna go gerra job, you layabout?' shouted the she-cat. She looked furious.

The tom was sniffing on a fish bone. 'I'll gerra job, don't you worry! Your goddam nagging ain't helping.'

'Twenny-two hours you sleep for, you don't do nuffink round 'ere. Nuffink.'

Douglas straightened his back. 'Uh, hello there, Douglas Schnitty here, your local MP.'

'I know who you are,' she snapped. 'What d'ya want?'

The tom slunk off.

'Sorry to bother you, I know this is a tough time. I have come here to listen, to take your story to the Prime Minister.'

Marjorie was still ignoring his repeated requests to meet. Showed how much she cared. But he had another idea — perhaps she could appoint him as Minister for the Homeless; he would make it his mission to lift 100,000 cats out of the bins within six months. He would type out a proposal today. 'Can I, uh, ask why you have ended up here?'

'Pfft. What cannai say? I was a cleaner in the hospital, me hubby hunted mice and sold it at a premium, we was doing awight. We was 'appy wiv our lot. Next fing, he loses 'is business, we lose our 'ome, and we's in the slums.'

'I am so sorry to hear that.'

'I was hoping for change wiv this Marjorie, and wiv you lot, I voted for yous. I mean I'd 'ave preferred it if she weren't a moggy, but I looked past that.'

Douglas glanced around. There must have been about 40 cats crammed in the slum. It was the newest one in his constituency. It had only appeared yesterday.

'Thank goodness your husband is good at hunting —'

'Yeah! I sure as hell ain't. I make a lousy hunter. Was never any good arrit, and nobody bovvered to show me.'

'Yes, that's a big problem nowadays,' said Douglas. 'At least we've finally put it back on the school curriculum.'

'I bet you is quite the hunter and all, wiv your toned body and that.'

Douglas looked away and smiled broadly. 'I get by, I suppose.'

The she-cat came closer and examined him. 'You look more like an athlete than a politician.'

'Why, thank you,' mumbled Douglas. 'I swim every night, you know.'

'I've always wanted to be good at swimmin'. Maybe you can teach me one of these days.' She had a mischievous glower in her eyes. Douglas felt himself getting aroused.

'I'm sure we can work something out.'

The she-cat slow-blinked at him. 'I'll be the perfec' student.'

He looked away again. What the hell was he doing? He

was here to help her, not break up her bloody marriage.

'Look, I'm grateful that you voted for us, ma'am. How do you think Marjorie is performing overall?'

'Not convinced if I'm honest, and that's nuffink to do wiv her being a moggy. I get that she has to bring in all these cuts and fings, not sure 'ow that's meant to help us out here in the bins, though. They're gonna hurt us. We need 'elp too.'

Well, this was embarrassing, Douglas thought. She was absolutely right. And what the hell was he supposed to say to her now? How could he justify the damn cuts? This was Marjorie's fault. She clearly didn't care.

He found himself looking away once again in the short encounter. 'Listen, I, uh, agree. We need to get you inside some tree accommodation. Quickly.'

'We're on the waiting lists and that. 'Ere, do you know who'd make a great leader? That Hector bloke.'

'Hector Perp Pahpousson? The Defence Secretary?'

'Yeah, he's got summink about him. Speaks his mind about low taxes and funding the military and that. I like 'im a lot.'

'Really?'

'Yeah, you'll find he's very popular round these parts.'

'Wow. Well, look, I must get going. Have an urgent proposal to work on. But here…' He fumbled in his satchel. 'Take some of these kippers. They should see you through for a while.'

'Aw, fanks. Bless you.' She licked him on the chops. 'An' don't forget our swimmin' date!'

Douglas slunk off. He would give the Prime Minister one more chance to do the right thing.

A BROUHAHA
OVER NOTHING

There was Hector was slumped on his piano stool, his chubby head resting on a thick encyclopaedia of the greatest poets that ever lived. *Carmina Burana* thundered out of the speakers.

They had just watched the Siberian Cat army general finish an incoherent press conference, ranting about weak and malign foreign influences. It was that General Bulgakov, a grubby looking bloke with a maddened look in his eyes. He had been standing in front of a map of Europe. Britain was crossed out in red ink, or perhaps it was blood. The image was doing the rounds on social media.

'The only way to deal with him is through shock diplomacy, you know,' shouted Hector.

'Yeah, put him back in his box!' shouted Douglas over the deafening roar of the medieval chorus.

'A little hellfire raining on his parade will soon quieten him down,' shouted Hector.

'The prat won't know what's hit him,' shouted Douglas.

Hector shoved his spit sodden nip leaf in Douglas' face. Douglas politely declined.

'Shame our once great army has declined into a laughing-stock,' Hector continued. 'Morale is rock bottom, and that Bulgakov chap knows it.'

The great cantata finished, and Douglas jumped on the rare moment of quiet in his pal's office. 'Uh, Hec, listen, could I stay with you for a couple of nights? My, uh, well, we're getting renovations done at the mansion and the thing is —'

'Yahhp, not a problem! You know...' he went on with nip-leaf enthusiasm, 'we need a hundred billion British Mew cash injection into our defences. Shame the Prime Minister and her foolish Emergency Money Saving Committee do not understand the gravity of the situation.'

'Uh, a hundred billion British Mews, Hec? Sounds like rather a lot.'

'Yahhp! At the very least!'

'Maybe the poor sods living in the slums could have a little chunk of that,' said Douglas.

'You know,' Hector went on with energy from what had likely been a very generous moonshot lunch, 'she's made a grave error in not asking me to join her committee.'

'You're better than her crummy committee, Hec.'

'Yahhp! It doesn't matter, I would have politely declined anyway.'

'Uh, Hec, going back to staying with you, it's just for a couple of nights. And it's purely because —'

'Yahhp, yahhp, you are very welcome, sir! You know...' he went on, narrowing his bright blue eyes, 'the last thing this country needs is yet another useless committee. It's nothing more than a fat turkey —'

'A fat turkey stuffed full of career politicians,' said Douglas.

'Yahhp! A fat turkey stuffed with career politicians, nodding tomcats, and appeasers.'

The two bumped heads in affection. 'I'm inspired, Douggy. If I were in charge, I would pump billions into defence and build that state-of-the-art border wall. Think of the jobs that would be created, all those skilled construction cat workers building something their kittens, and kitten's kittens would be proud of —'

'Don't forget about the slum cats, Hec. They could do with some of those billions too, it's dire out there —'

'And I would slash their taxes,' Hector went on, in his own little world. 'I would fight the corner of our heroic troops and hardworking construction workers serving this country.'

'Perhaps we could recruit some of the slum cats into the army? Pay them handsomely —'

'Pardon me, Douggy, I didn't offer you any cream. Help yourself!'

'Thanks, Hec,' Douglas licked his lips. 'Listen, let's discuss all this properly when I come and stay with you. When suits?'

'All about the good old free market economics, I am,' Hector continued.

'Uh, yes, evidently,' said Douglas.

'I need to ask you something, sir!'

Perhaps he was deaf, thought Douglas.

'The esteemed Countryside Society needs a guest speaker to open their 100th anniversary gala next week.'

'Gosh. I'm flattered, Hec, but —'

'But our glorious leader, has banned me, yes banned

me, from giving any speeches or interviews outside of my ministerial brief. Well? Should I do it?'

'Oh. Well, I mean —'

'OK, OK, I'll do it! The countryside is a big deal in my constituency. The Society has money and influence; I need them on side. Perhaps I can persuade them to write a meaty cheque for a border wall, after all they won't want foreign strays infiltrating our green and pleasant land.'

'Doubt they'd want any slums popping up on our green and pleasant land either —'

'I will do it, yes!'

'Great, can you get a few bob out of them for the homeless too?'

'I don't see why not, sir! Anything is possible with a little Hector charm! I will respond to them immediately. That'll teach the Prime Minister to leave me out of her precious little committee. And the overpaid suits in her office, they can damn well —'

'They can go take a hike!' Douglas said. He got up and made some lame excuse about being late for the plumber. He had to be out of the mansion in a few hours, luckily Jitters had agreed to put him up tonight.

Hector gave him a lick. 'Oh, and come and stay whenever you like!'

'Thanks, pal. Grateful.'

'And bring your wonderful wife!'

'Uh, sure.'

'She's more than welcome to sample my special cream!'

'Uh, OK, Hec.'

*

Hector couldn't sleep. He flicked through his prized book: *1,000 eloquent words for a tomcat of serious social standing.* The opening speech for the Countryside Alliance was a big moment for him, he needed to impress. And just like every speech he delivered, he challenged himself to throw in one of the long words somewhere in his closing remarks.

He tried Douglas on his mobile for the fourth time. 'Ah, greetings, chap. I was wondering whether you were screening my calls for a moment.'

There was silence.

'Listen, I need a standout word to wow my Countryside Alliance audience.'

He heard his friend on the other end rabbiting on about having to make it quick, lots to do, blah, blah, blah.

'Yahhp! How about brouhaha? As in, "what a brouhaha over nothing". Or as in, "my excellent speech will cause a brouhaha in the Prime Minister's office".'

'Sure, why not?' came the hurried reply from his pal.

'How about lollygag?' As in, "we must stop lollygagging for the sake of our children!" Or "the Prime Minister's office is a bunch of slackers, lollygaggers!" Pa-hah!'

'I've got to go,' said Douglas.

'What?' He grabbed a mirror and admired his fine long whiskers.

'Ah hah!' he continued. 'For nothing! Flocci – for nothing, nauci – for nothing, nihili – for nothing, pilifi – for nothing —'

'What?' said Douglas this time.

'As in, "we must be bold, and blunt, and reckless, and shameless in protecting our glorious countryside otherwise our work will be… floccinaucinihilipilification.'

'I think you have a winner there, Hec.'

'Yahhp! Must scoot now, I have things to do, ta-tah.' The Defence Secretary hung up.

For nothing, Hector mused. Worthless, not important, much like the Prime Minister and her Emergency Money Saving Committee. It would be a doddle to topple her. He was a cat of serious standing in the Party, a rockstar amongst the grassroots. Colleagues would put in letters of no confidence tomorrow under his instruction. Especially in return for a bowl of cream. It would soon be time to turn things up a notch, time to let off some fireworks. The country would soon be free from the grimy paws of Marjorie.

Floccinaucinihilipilification. He ripped the word out of his book, rolled it up carefully and stuffed it under his collar. He drifted off into a well-earned snooze.

WELFARE, A
HOOMANIAN CONCEPT.

Jitters and his ma had gone to bed. Douglas lay awake in their guest room. His first night without his mansion. His first night of the rest of his life. It would be tough, but he was a fighter. He would endure.

He'd had a fun few hours. He absolutely loved the mother. Maples. She'd spent the evening complimenting the ginger markings on his neck and chest, saying how gorgeous they were. She'd complimented his brown leather brogues. They were only for special occasions, he'd told her, to purrs of approval. The more moonshot she supped down, the more flirtatious she became. She even pecked him on the lips at one stage. She would have been quite the looker back in the day, Douglas concluded.

They had tucked into a homemade Sicilian fish soup, cooked from scratch by a very excited Jitters. He'd spent the evening oblivious to his mother's playful behaviour and feeling the need to announce what he was doing at every stage. This time he'd tried frying the fillet of halibut and prawns first, rather than just boiling everything straight. He had added in chopped parsley and lemon juice. The heat was

36

kept low throughout, optimum for allowing the flavours to interact and dance with each other, apparently. Yes, Douglas had been paying attention. He had no choice in the matter. It was a very vibrant and impressive dish, nonetheless.

Clang! The minister for welfare and sums bumped into something and appeared out of nowhere.

'Uh, Jitters, everything OK?'

The grey cat was jabbing away on his phone, muttering to himself. Something about a new strategy on CatKiss. It was a numbers game, he said in a daze. He would send slow blinks to more she-cats, he told himself.

'Jitters, are you OK?' Douglas asked again.

'S-S-Still no response from that c-c-cute one with the p-p-pointy ears. Is it because I'm a F-F-Freedom Cat? Not the first t-t-time I've been g-g-ghosted for being a F-F-Freedom Cat.' Jitters hissed.

He seemed to be in his own little world. In some sort of bizarre trance.

'Perhaps it's the p-p-profile pic. But I like the s-s-selfie with ma, shows I'm g-g-grounded. A family cat.'

What the hell was happening? Douglas had read somewhere that you should never awaken a sleep-walking cat. Not if you valued your life.

'Leave me a-a-alone, you b-b-bastard!' he shouted.

Blimey, that escalated quickly. Who on earth could he be talking to?

The pent up grey cat turned and faced Douglas. 'I will s-s-stay loyal to her!' he screamed. 'You are nothing more than a d-d-dirty little schemer!'

'Shh, settle down, Jitters,' whispered Douglas.

Jitters flinched and looked straight into Douglas' eyes. He looked a right state.

'D-D-Douglas? Everything a-a-alright?'

He was back, thank God. And there was Maples behind him, looking concerned.

'All fine, Jitters. Think you may have been, uh, sleepwalking.'

This little arrangement wasn't working out.

✶

An hour later, Jitters was back in his office. He was sitting in his rooftop garden, the "green room" as he liked to call it, the cubbyhole at the highest point in his work space. He chewed on the grass he was growing, it was soft and luscious. It helped chill him out, relax from the stresses of the job. And his terrible love life.

He got to work. He had been informed that Britain was weeks away from defaulting on its debt to the *International Feline Prosperity Fund*, and that made him nervous. It would be the first time a developed nation would do so since the extinction of the hoomans. The PM had called him yesterday and asked for emergency measures to announce imminently. She had sounded panicked. He went back over the policy paper he had written on the introduction of a benefits cap.

'It's not f-f-fair that cats *in* work can earn more than c-c-cats *out* of work,' he announced.

'I mean cats *out* of w-w-w-work earning more than cats *in* work… that's not fair.'

Suggest capping benefits to 500 British Mews per month, per family, he jotted down in his little black book. *It will save millions which can be used to pay off our debts.*

He'd done the sums and they added up. He knew he'd be accused of balancing the books on the backs of the poor. He nervously twitched his tail.

'We must eliminate our d-d-debts!' he declared.

'C-C-Cut them!' he shouted to loud imaginary cheers.

'Slash them!' They looked at him lovingly.

'No more giving away m-m-m-millions to foreign governments just in interest p-p-payments!' he cried.

'No more open chequebooks for our f-f-f-families!'

He scrambled around the green room. 'I m-m-mean open chequebooks for out of work families. We don't want those. No.'

He plonked onto his side. Welfare was such a hoomanian concept. He thought of his ma. She brought him up just fine as a single mother, made sure he had everything he could ever need. And she didn't take a single British Mew from the state. It was time to wean ourselves off it, for the sake of our kittens.

'It must p-p-p-pay to be out of work. *In* work! Yes. Damn it.'

He refreshed his CatKiss and zoomed in on his profile pic. He would keep it, he decided. It demonstrated he was a cat of strong family values. He highlighted and deleted his long biog, nobody cared about his favourite food or TV programmes. Or how he took his milk. He typed: *On a mission to slash UK debt.* That would do it. Much more impactful. Showed he had some depth about him, and a lifesaving job.

He decided to call it a day. He would stay loyal to the Prime Minister, no matter what the likes of Hector were scheming. He had an opportunity to impress her, and change the country for the better. He'd come so far over the years. He put his rucksack on and sauntered out of his office. Tail up and contented. 'Maow.'

August 2009

'Your turn, Jitters,' said the stern headmistress, Mrs Debonaire. The class had been reciting *My Friend the Rat* in the stifling summer heat. The hall went silent, and he could feel the eyes on him. He heard sniggering in the distance.

'Have you-you... seen my friend...

Billy the rat?

He sat on... on the h-h-hat...'

'No, Jitters!' scolded the headmistress.

The class burst out laughing. Jitters wanted to hide.

'Now one more chance, Jitters, from the top please.'

Jitters could feel the sweat sticking under his paws. He wished his ma was sitting next to him.

'Have y-y-you s-s-s-seen my friend...

B-B-B-illy the rat?

He s-s-s-sat on the... the red h-h-h-at...'

'That's it, Jitters, in the corner now! Get yourself into the lead!'

Oh no, not the punishment lead again. Jitters walked to the front of the hall, head down in shame. The headmistress tied the leather punishment lead to his collar, shaking her head in disappointment. He was to stand facing the wall, in front of everyone, for the remaining 15 minutes of the lesson.

'Now then, Caroline, your turn.'

'Have you seen my friend
Billy the rat?
He sat on the mat
With a big red hat.'

'Excellent, Caroline, well done!'

HOSPITALITY AT
HECTOR'S

Douglas was stuffed. He attempted one more glug of cream, the best cream he'd ever tasted. The special thick cream that had been lovingly made for generations by the Pahpoussons. It was flowing down an enormous cream fountain, the centre piece of Hector's reception room. Douglas watched on in awe at the velvety good stuff coming down the enormous rotating gold-plated tiers. This thing was even bigger than the one in his office, it was at least 10 feet tall. Tacky red neon letters next to it flashed: *It's cream o'clock!*

Hector sat draped in a blanket. It had the "eyes and claws" on it. It was the eighth national flag Douglas had spotted in the mansion. The watchful yellow eyes seemed to be following him around the place.

The Defence Secretary swigged the last of his moonshot and threw his empty bowl into the crackling fire. *SMASH!* He had spent the last half an hour lecturing Douglas on the intricacies of various moonshot and cream pairings and which combinations were a no-no.

'Say, where's your beautiful wife?'

'Uh, she's, uh, staying with a friend,' said Douglas. 'Listen,

Hec, you and I should get together and force some money out of the PM somehow for —'

'Ah, yahhp, for our heroic troops!'

'And for the homeless, Hec. We've got to get them out of the bins.'

'Say, Douggy, we should write to her, give her an ultimatum, send it to *The Meowington Times*.'

'An ultimatum?'

'We put her on notice, make it clear her days are numbered unless she commits the required funding for our troops.'

'Bit premature, no, Hec?'

'What?'

'Giving her an ultimatum without exploring —'

'Think of it as a warning shot. We demand a hundred billion British Mews or else. Give her five days. That sort of thing.'

Douglas was flagging. His attention shifted to his paws. They'd never felt so snug, in Hector's special guest slippers. Furry slippers and the finest cream paired with moonshot, decadence at its best.

'Leave it with me, sir! I'll draft something overnight. A public ransom note. Signed by you and me.'

'Uh, —'

'Also, I've been thinking, perhaps it's time we paid that General Bulgakov a little visit.'

'We?'

'Yahhp! Just the two of us, dear chap! I, the military cat, and you with your dashing looks. A winning combination! I'll do the talking.'

'Why would we do that?'

'Element of surprise, of course! I'd be the first western minister to ever meet him. In the spirit of negotiation. Friendship. Something like that.'

'But we're not his friends?'

'It's all about the psychological operations!'

'OK, Hec.'

'We need to be unpredictable! Keep him guessing. Keep him asking "what will we do next?"'

'OK, Hec, I'm knackered though, time for a kip?'

'Yahhp, yahhp, plenty of time for a kip, don't you worry. Are you free next week, per chance?'

'Let's see, Hec. I'll, uh, check my diary.'

'We can travel first class!'

'Sounds lovely. Must hit the hay though.' Douglas rose.

'Make yourself comfortable in any of the nine rooms, sir! And keep those bags packed! We'll soon be off to Russia!'

Douglas trotted out as fast as he could.

"Think of the photo opportunity, Douggy!'

MOVING IN DAY

Douglas prowled up and down in his underground den. His head was spinning after the antics at Hector's. Shame it hadn't worked out over there, the mansion was incredible, but that guy was too much at times. There was no way he was signing any public ransom note to the Prime Minister nor would he be flying to Russia any time soon. Moving into the office for a while would be his best option.

He unpacked the fish food. 10 British Mews for a measly batch of freeze-dried flakes; who knew feeding the fish would be so expensive? He got to work arranging the tubs in a precarious pile beside his files of constituency casework. He took out the precious packages of nip leaf next and shoved them out of sight behind the fish food.

He crept over to the clownfish. He'd just collected her from the mansion. 'Don't worry,' he whispered, 'we'll be OK here. I guess we're, uh, office buddies now.'

He kept his eyes fixed onto his friend, his confidant. She was doing her little dance again, wiggling to and fro. She had polished off her dinner. 'Well done, Shuffles.'

He splashed his paw in her salt water. He liked the cool sensation.

'I'll make sure you're OK.' He didn't know what he would

do without his bright orange friend. He cast his mind back to the night he'd rescued her from the river on one of his nightly swims. She had looked so hungry, almost dead. He took her in and nursed her back to health. His ex had mocked him. Said the fish wouldn't last past breakfast with him. Well, she'd been proved wrong. Shuffles had been his therapy fish, his constant through everything that had happened.

Douglas sharpened his claws on the bare wall. He felt the heat of the bright yellow bulb, just about hanging onto the frayed wire. He could do with some soft furnishings round the place, some colour, some warmth. And some air freshener; it smelt stale.

'Can you believe it, Shuffles? I never ever saw her in anything but the finest attire. She was a classy one, a catess through and through. She was a bloody snob if I'm honest, and yet she turns up to court in raggedy clothes. They probably weren't even hers. And those judges fell for it hook, line, and sinker.'

He rummaged through his hotchpotch pile of laundry; his shirts stank. He would wash them in the river tonight.

'And what possibly could that bastard judge have been whispering to her? They looked rather chummy, they did me over, Shuffles. They did me over real good.'

He remembered the envelope he had picked up as he left the mansion for the last time. *FINAL DEMAND,* it said in red ink. *Purrfect outcomes every time,* read the squiggly text at the bottom. He slit it open with his teeth.

Dear Mr Schnitty,

Please find attached a breakdown of your legal fees totalling 10,000 British Mews. It would be appreciated if you could make payment in full within seven days.

Kindest,

Your pawsitive legal team

Well, that would wipe out any savings he had left, and for what? Perhaps if his dope of a lawyer hadn't snoozed through most of the proceedings, she wouldn't have ended up with everything. He couldn't even be bothered to show up for the damn judgement.

Douglas felt exhausted. He lay on the dirty rug that he'd found on the side of the road. The dust from it made him sneeze. It fit perfectly in his new abode after he'd folded it in half. He stretched out, knocking the pile of fish food everywhere.

FOR WE ARE CATS

He looked up at his tiny television. It was on its last legs, like the rest of the joint. The Prime Minister was about to begin her impromptu press conference. It was called two hours ago.

He picked up a stub of chalk and scratched *518,964* on the wall. He took his time forming the numbers and stared for a while. 'More than half a million cats homeless and living in the bins,' he murmured. 'Let that sink in.' Thank goodness, he wasn't one of them; his poky little office saving him by the skin of his teeth. Still nothing from the Prime Minister on his idea of a minister for the homeless.

The new dental sticks advert was playing on the box. 'Look after your gnashers with our chick-chick-chicken and cat nip deeental stiiicks,' howled an operatic voice. The annoying advert cut abruptly to a well-groomed pure white moggy. She trotted to the podium, paused awkwardly, and leapt up. She was wearing a red leather collar with shiny little beads on it. Looked like a supermarket job, CatSaver, just like that Mandy from the bins had said. It did look a bit tacky come to think of it.

'Good evening, Marjorie Wilson here,' announced the Prime Minister. 'You can call me Marj. I'm just a normal cat, like you.' Her tail was casually hanging.

'Oh God,' muttered Douglas.

'Tonight, I want to, I mean, I, er… *wanna*, outline, a package of emergency measures, for we are almost bankrupt. *Skint,* one could say.'

This was her trying to be down with the kids again. 'I have inherited the largest debt of any major economy. One in every four British Mews we spend is being borrowed. It's unacceptable, I mean, er… it's *mad*.'

Mad? Seriously, Prime Minister?

She supped noisily on some water. 'The truth is we're facing a national emergency. In the last six months alone, over a thousand businesses have folded. Thousands of cats have, er… lost their homes and they are living in the bins because there's no social housing left. Our tree estates are, er… *chocka*.'

Her paws were shaking. 'The last lot in power tried this unnatural concept of welfare. It was also tried by the hoomans many generations ago. It failed back then, and it's failed now. It's bad, it's, er… well, it's *wack*.'

Douglas winced. She needed a serious talking to.

'Do you know we are spending, er… hang on, er…'

This was beyond embarrassing.

'Er… 192 billion British Mews on welfare today? All that crazy amount of money is going on the unemployed and on social housing tenants in the tree estates while the homeless living in bins are literally left to starve and, er… well, fend for themselves.'

'Yes!' shouted Douglas. 'Finally something about the homeless! Hallelujah! What are you going to do about it, PM?'

Marjorie glanced around nervously, her right ear twitching.

'We must tackle our ballooning welfare bill. Spending tens of billions on benefits cannot continue, for we are cats, and we are a strong and proud community. My government will, er...'

'Well, spit it out then!' Douglas hissed.

'Er, make sure it pays to work.'

Douglas hissed some more.

The Prime Minister stared awkwardly back at him. 'Thanks to the last government, there are families living in tree estates receiving 2,000 British Mews every month in benefits. This is outrageous. We will not abolish welfare, but we will for the first time introduce a maximum limit of 500 British Mews per family, per month. That's, er... that's rather generous. *Well generous.*'

'*Well generous*?' yelled Douglas. 'Really?' Shuffles was observing from the safety of her tank.

She droned on. 'We have hard choices to make. We will become a lot more productive as a country if we double our working day from two to four hours. That's why I will also be writing to the President of the Global Cats Alliance to say that we will ditch this ridiculous Rule of 18; that is of course the right to a guaranteed, er... well, 18 hours of sleep a day.'

'She's done for,' whispered Douglas. 'The masses won't tolerate that.'

Marjorie froze suddenly, looking as if she'd forgotten her lines. She shifted uncomfortably, her twitching ears in overdrive. She went on after a long pause. 'If we sleep for, er, say, 16 hours, and work for four hours, we still have, er... er...'

'Four goddamn hours!' screamed Douglas.

'Well, we will have four hours for sports and leisure activities. I-I myself manage on just 14 hours of sleep, and I manage to juggle a demanding job.'

'Perhaps if she slept more, she'd be able to string a sentence together,' Douglas remarked.

'And we need to think like cats again. Er... who's, er, who's with me?'

The pause was excruciating. 'This should start at kittenhood. On my first day in office, I introduced compulsory hunting practice in our nurseries. And today I am going further and announcing that we will increase that hunting practice from 10 to, er... well, to 15 minutes a day.'

'Well, that's the best thing I've heard so far,' Douglas mumbled.

'And once we pay off our debts and help the homeless out of the bins, I will cut your taxes bit by bit so you can keep more of your hard-earned money. For we are cats, and we should have the means to, er... well, to fend for ourselves and our families first and foremost.'

'Tax cuts? Seriously? And how the hell are you going to pay for them?' growled Douglas.

'Let me, I mean, er... *lemme* remind you, 54 years ago, yes, three lifetimes ago, the hoomans became extinct after running out of money and food. They couldn't even feed their children in the end because of their poor choices. The Cats Collective haven't learnt any lessons. We must take the difficult decisions now if we are to rescue ourselves. I will make sure we live like cats once again. Thank you, or rather, er, well... *peace out.*'

Douglas wandered over to the precarious stack of fish food, and carefully edged out his burner phone from behind, with the tip of his paw. He switched it on and began typing:

> Angus, this PM won't last the full term. Her reckless cuts and disregard for the needy will finish her off. Besides, there is a long line of suitors for the top job. Some of them smarter and much more sensible. No amount of urban parlance or tacky collars from CatSaver can save her. Anon.

He felt depressed at the thought of the homeless living in the bins. He'd met so many successful and interesting cats on his nightly rounds this week, the chef with the wonky nose, the vet, the lawyer couple, the cleaner and her hunter husband, and of course Mandy. All of them had lost everything very suddenly in the economic crash. They were desperate, yet astoundingly many of them were still giving Marjorie the benefit of the doubt. But these cuts would not help them. He knew what it was like, he had almost lost everything too. He came into politics to help the situation, not make it worse. He'd be damned if he was going to let her get away with it. She needed to go.

He licked the cream off his lips. He had overdone it on his eclair at tea and felt sick. He hit send.

*

Hector turned off his gold-plated TV and poured himself an early hour moonshot. Rich, intense and a deep yellow in appearance. Straight, on the rocks. Embarrassing and incoherent, he concluded. *And not a single word about our military. Wilfully deaf to the grave threats coming from a mere 1,500 miles to the east of us. I blush on her behalf!*

He realised he'd come to work in his golden silk pyjamas, but he didn't care. He felt comfy in them. So very present and in the moment. And they looked regal. He peered up to the press cutting of his recent summit with his Danish counterpart. He had worn the very same pyjamas, and she was looking at him in awe. Perhaps he would send her a pair and set a trend in Scandinavia. Wah!

He knocked back some moonshot. It was helping numb the anxiety. He supped some more and was well on his way to a snooze.

January 2008

'Pahpousson! Get up here now!' screamed the Major. The wide-eyed youngster leapt up. He strode confidently in front of his new peers. It was time to sharpen up. This was no longer boarding school; slouching and skiving would not be tolerated. *Clang!* A broomstick hit his head and fell onto the floor. 'Take position!' the Major ordered. He had to pick up the thing, pretend it was a rifle, and point it at pigeons and various flying objects. They couldn't even afford to provide an actual rifle to train him.

Hey-ho, it still beat the two-hour "inclusion session" he had to sit through on day one. He got a bollocking for referring to the invading Persians as "they" and "them" in some bizarre roleplay. That's what you got with the Cats Collective in power.

He recalled opening his diversity class test results over breakfast on day two. *PAHPOUSSON FINAL SCORE 0/10. FAIL!* He went on to score a zero in the next one, and a two in the one after that. Luckily, the diversity lecturer was open to bribes from a certain Lord and Lady Pahpousson. Well, in fairness, the political game and the cream manufacturing business on the side had been kind to them over the years. They needed something to spend their fortune on.

He remembered phoning his mamma and pappa every day. 'Pa-paaah, I really think I should come home and put my mind to better uses.'

'No way, kid, not an option. The army will make a serious tomcat out of you.'

'I beg you, Pa-paaaah. I detest this place.'

He couldn't believe he had lasted a year. His morale had bombed quicker than the dodgy chopper that had almost killed him. Crap equipment, fake weapons, rusty tanks. That was business as usual under the Collective lot; he didn't expect the same under a Freedom Cat Prime Minister. She needed to go.

A ROLLOCKING

Waoow! Hector bolted under his desk dodging the copy of *The Meowington Times* flying towards him. He peeped out to see Fee glaring at him with her beady green eyes.

'What the hell is this headline?' she shrieked.

Hector peeked over at the paper and caught the splash in big letters, *UK Defence Secretary: Grow a backbone and stand up against Siberian scoundrels!*

'Ah. Well, um, yes. The thing is…'

'I told you you're not allowed to speak to the press, you absolute lunatic!' screamed Fee.

'What?'

'You agreed not to speak to the press, remember?'

'Did I? Well, I must say the headline is a tad misleading —'

His press advisor growled and made a lunge towards him. She was looking especially tired and scruffy of late. Maybe she needed some of his extra strong nip leaf to chill her out.

'I was only talking about the latest intelligence I had received,' he continued.

'What the hell are voters going to think? Also, nobody sane will back your big idea to build a wall!'

'Yes, they will,' Hector muttered. 'I'm the only one with the cajones to say things that the majority secretly agree with. It's what sets me apart from the bland, career orientated —'

'But you do realise that we are an island?'

'What's that?'

'We are a bloody island!'

'So?'

'And our species can climb pretty damn well?'

'Well, they won't dare if we plant cacti along the top. He missed out that vital piece of —'

'And how many times have I told you that you cannot say the "S" word! Saying you want to keep the "strays" out is not socially acceptable anymore!' Fee's squeal got louder.

'Pah! Utterly ridiculous. Political correctness, it's gone bananas.'

It was true, he thought. We became a nation of softies with the Cats Collective in power, and if anything, it was only getting worse with Marjorie as Prime Minister. He'd seen the scourge of political correctness spread in the army. Poor recruits being lectured on diversity and the importance of expressing emotions rather than the art of combat and victory. That General Bulgakov must be retching with laughter.

He glanced over at her. She was rabbiting on about immigration being Home Office business. Mustn't stray from the Defence brief, she lectured. How come it was OK for her to use the "S" word?

'And whilst we're at it,' she continued, 'nobody is going to pay us to sponsor our empty trees. It would be a crap investment.'

'What?'

'You heard me, Hector. Why wouldn't we just renovate them and use them for desperately needed social housing? You know, for our own population?'

'My idea will raise us billions for the military. World peace will only be achieved through our display of strength. Alas the bloody Prime Minister refuses to listen. But don't you worry, my dear, I have a plan. I will see to it that she is removed from office.'

Fee bared her teeth.

Hector slipped away behind the mahogany table leg. He had a thumping headache. *Maybe, just maybe, she won't see me here.*

'I can see you, you idiot!'

THE BLACK
CATS SOCIETY

Douglas scratched three times on the rustic pine door. A rusty sign read: *Private, enter at your peril.* He prowled nonchalantly in a circle and scratched three more times. It was precisely two minutes to midnight. The door creaked ajar, and Douglas slipped through the gap.

He hobbled down the steep and windy steps. Hundreds of bright candles of all shapes and sizes lit up the lair. The smell of wax calmed his nerves, it was a good distraction from his stiff neck. He hadn't managed a decent kip since moving into the office, having to squish into his four by four cell alongside Shuffles. His nostrils felt as if they were crammed with dust mites.

Black cats lay to his left, to his right, and up above him as he trotted through the aisle. There were some eighty cats in the lair purring, sipping away, and scribbling notes on what they were tasting. Douglas took his usual spot towards the front on the left.

'What's that you have, then?' whispered a black Chinchilla

next to him. Douglas instantly recognised his tubby pal, and his unmissable golden pyjamas.

'Ha-choo! Greetings, Hector! 20-year-old moonshot, extremely rare.'

'Fabulous. Peat?'

'No, ha-choo! Extremely smooth and velvety on the palate. And you?'

Hector took a gulp. 'Peaty, from Kentucky. Caramelly. Medicinal.'

The strong stench of moonshot blended with the scent of candle wax to create a pleasant musky aroma. Douglas found it soothing in between his fits of sneezing.

'Say, Douggy, old chap, we never did send our ransom note to the PM.'

'Probably for the best, Hec.'

'Yahhp. We need to do something though. We are in quite a pickle, don't you think?'

'Yes, we're moving in the wrong direction with this cuts malarkey. The slum cats are suffering and thousands more will end up living in the bins. Most of them can't even hunt thanks to our failing education system. We're screwed.'

'Yahhp, quite. And soon we'll all be speaking Russian.'

'Really?'

'The intelligence I'm receiving from our Maine Coon partners in Washington is sobering, Douggy. The Russian Blue and Siberian Cat armies have got hold of these missiles that travel faster than the speed of sound. I hear they've earmarked one or two just for us. A special present.'

'Jeez, that doesn't sound good.'

'Yahhp! They would pummel our towns and cities.'

'Definitely Marjorie's fault,' whispered Douglas. 'She's getting the big things wrong. She's not listening. She's becoming a disaster of a Prime Minister.'

'And she waffles on like a hoodlum. The time for writing notes has passed. We need to force her out!'

'Hmm, I suspect you may be right, Hec.'

'Yah, and then we could take over. You and me, sir! I would make you my Chancellor in a heartbeat!'

'Calm down, Hec, go easy. One thing at a time.'

Hector's tail started thrashing wildly. 'You know, we could strike, take her out!'

'Pardon?'

'Take her out, old chap, dispose of her.'

Douglas studied his pal. He needed to lay off the strong stuff.

'She'd be finished, gone!' continued Hector, teeth on display. 'Vamoosed.'

Loose talk. Drunken, loose talk, concluded the senior backbencher. 'Hmm, sounds mortifying.'

'It could be over quickly, Douggy.'

'You could give a press conference immediately afterwards,' Douglas egged him on. 'Why not lead the obituary in the *Daily Mog.*'

'Eugh! Not the failing *Daily Mog!*'

'Ha.'

'Listen, old chap, we could mount a special operation.'

Douglas rolled his eyes. 'Go on then, Hec… how exactly would we do that?'

'Well, militarily speaking, it would be quite feasible to put together a rather discreet device —'

'Uh-huh…'

'A teeny tiny little thing… we can smuggle the beauty into Downing Street when she's sleeping, and, er…'

'And, what exactly, Hec?'

'And, well, kaboom!' The lair fell silent.

'No, Hec. Don't be ridiculous! Nobody's blowing her up. And keep your voice down, will you? Someone will think you're being serious!'

Hector leaned in and whispered, 'All it would take is one call to my contacts in the military.'

'OK, Hec, enough. Go easy on the juice.'

A see-through pouch fell onto Hector's paws and gave him a fright. He sniffed at it. It seemed to be stuffed with some sort of chopped flower, bright orange in colour.

'Be careful with that,' came a whisper from behind. 'One teaspoon of the finely chopped tiger lily will do the trick. Sprinkle it over her food.' They both looked around. The shadowy character had disappeared.

'Yikes! We could mix it up with some of the extra strong cat nip. You know, the special stuff —'

'Keep your paws off that, Hec. And keep your flipping voice down, you're going to land us in it.'

The Defence Secretary shoved his face into a cream pie. 'She wouldn't suspect a thing,' he said, mouth stuffed and bits flying everywhere.

'We're not poisoning the Prime Minister, Hec, and we're not blowing her up. Not quite what I had in mind.'

He could be such a fucking idiot sometimes. He needed to watch himself, even if he was bluffing.

It was five minutes to four in the morning. The Black

Cats Society proceeded to open their meeting after hours of gossip, moonshot and naps.

> *Huh-hum-huh-huh*
> *Huh-hum-huh-huh.*

> *We sit strong and proud*
> *We see things nobody sees.*

> *We feast like kings*
> *We make our Mews*
> *We fend for ourselves.*

> *We're everywhere you look*
> *And we're nowhere to be found.*

> *Om-yah-mew-mew*
> *Biladi, Katze, Mao.*

> *Huh-hum-huh-huh*
> *Huh-hum-huh-huh.*

The traditional chant got louder and louder and ended abruptly at the clash of two giant cymbals. Silence fell across the lair. Mukerjee, the serious and frail looking Society elder, made his way slowly to the front.

'Before we concern ourselves with the dirt on the opposition leader, let's hear what sightings and intelligence we have gathered on Operation Snowflake!'

Hector sniggered. 'Snowflake! I came up with that code

name for our glorious leader, you know. Bloody marvellous.'

'Remember,' Mukerjee continued, 'she may be one of us, but it's important we keep an eye on her too, keep her in her place. It's for the best.'

A character in the corner started ranting about the embarrassment of having a moggy in charge of the country. 'We are a laughing stock at home and abroad, I tell you.'

'Hear, hear!' shouted Hector, swigging more moonshot.

'Shh, Hec,' whispered Douglas. The idiot couldn't handle his drink.

'Did you know, I spotted her tucking into some CatSaver Basic biscuits the other day. They stunk out the canteen! No class!' moaned a skinny she-cat at the back.

'Quite!' came a response. 'And she looks so unhealthy, so tired, and a bit podgy if you ask me.'

Somebody else piped up about having dug into her family's tax affairs and having found discrepancies. 'The thing is, upon initial scrutiny, I am not at all certain that they should have even qualified for social housing when Marjorie was a kitten,' droned the low-pitched voice.

Hector had fallen asleep in a puddle of moonshot.

LATE FOR DUTY

That night inside Parliament, Jitters was reclining on a silk cushion in Committee Corridor, and he was feeling on top of the world. He was browsing romantic getaways. He had been on a date, and it couldn't have gone any better. They had really connected, they shared a fish pie after a few moonshots, and she even let him kiss her outside the Tube station before they parted ways. She was a gorgeous slim moggy, super intelligent, and he liked the way she kept licking her upper lip. 'Oh, Jitsy, you can do better than a moggy,' his ma would probably tell him. She would change her mind once they met, he was sure of it.

Perhaps he would whisk her away to the luxury hotel in Cornwall, where he had recently taken his ma for her surprise birthday weekend. That was a great weekend; his ma loved being on the coast, it made her so happy. They had paddled in the sea, climbed the famous Bedruthan Steps, and napped under the stars to their hearts' content. Might be a bit strange to take a date to the same place. Neither needed to know.

He looked at his watch. 4.21am. Damn it, he had lost track of time. He was meant to be over in Downing Street, doing his duty and guarding the Prime Minister. There was still time to make it, she would probably still be asleep. She was vulnerable after all, just like his ma used to be. There were too many aggressive types about in Parliament. Too many around her that wanted her to fail. *Snakes.*

A ginger moggy with a gravelly voice gave him a fright, just as he was packing up. It was that Kranken, the leader of the opposition. 'What the hell is wrong with you, Ophelia — why didn't you mention you'd bought a bloody three-million-British-Mew mansion? And that too in Kensington?'

'But… but —' whimpered the young she-cat. She looked stunning.

'How's it gonna land with the public that we, the Cats Collective, wanna bring in a mansion tax? Yet the Shadow Health Secretary, who by the way is the loudest bloody critic of mansions and the posh twats living in them, buys one of the most expensive ones for herself?'

Ophelia backed away. 'But my little Portia was really set on the neighbourhood. She —'

'Yeah, but it's one of the most exclusive neighbourhoods in the goddam country, you know?' Kranken shouted.

'I did it for my Portia. She feels safe there, there's a real community feel. And the high street has a lot of independent shops —'

'Get out!' Kranken's angry voice echoed through the corridor.

'Fine, Ophelia is leaving, but this is not your corridor, Leader. And may I remind you that you hardly live in a tree estate yourself.'

'Why are you referring to yourself in the third cat, Ophelia? It sounds stupid. And by the way, I don't live in no bloody mansion!'

'And may I also remind you that every single cat in our shadow Cabinet lives in a mansion. Perhaps they are not quite mansions in a technical sense, but to the ordinary cat —'

'You're having a laugh! The toffs on the other side live in mansions, we're against them.'

'I think —'

'Listen, you're not to comment on this publicly. Keep your head down for the next few days, understand?'

'I beg your pardon?'

'Keep your head down and do NOT talk to press whatever you do.' Kranken disappeared into his office and slammed the door.

'I think you need to consider the nuances of the situation,' muttered Ophelia as she slunk off.

Jitters sprinted off to Downing Street. He couldn't believe what he'd just heard, it was dynamite.

FOCUS GROUP

About 200 or so Freedom Cat MPs were assembled in the Grand Committee room. Douglas was reclining in the corner at the back. He felt rough after the antics at the Society overnight. The moonshot was fading and his aches and pains were creeping back on him. He was late for his swim and desperate to get into the cool water. He couldn't for the life of him understand why the Prime Minister had called this sudden early morning meeting.

There she was, standing at the front of the room. Staring with a vacant look at her rather clunky and text-heavy slides on the screen. He squinted ahead and could make out something about a focus group. Why the hell was she conducting a focus group already? They had only been in power five minutes. Hector was leaning into him snoring, his sharp yellow front teeth visible.

Douglas gave him a sharp prod. 'Wake up, buddy, we need to talk.'

'Gah,' came the response.

'Look, you were being crazy last night. Go easy on the moonshot, OK?'

'Bwaah!' Hector shuddered. He rolled over and started snoring again.

'It's gonna land you in serious shit one of these days,' muttered Douglas.

'If I can please, er… well, please have your attention,' Marjorie began hesitantly. At least half the room was asleep, and the Commons cafeteria hadn't even opened. She had immediately launched herself into full-on lecture mode. 'We've must be attuned to public opinion, and we've must be prepared to, er… well, to listen to the hard truths.'

Public opinion, hard truths, blah blah blah, thought Douglas. *Sounds like she's planning an early election or something.*

'We've invested in the biggest focus group operation of its kind, some, er… er…'

Douglas clenched his paws.

'Er… 69 of them. Pretty much one in every city of the UK. And I must be frank with you, the results make dreadful reading for me.'

Crikey, 69 focus groups? She should get herself out into the real world, the bin cats would tell her a few truths for free. So much for being the Party of fiscal responsibility! Douglas felt sick.

'Six in ten of those polled view the Prime Minister, er, that's me then, as *uninspiring*.'

69 focus groups, thought Douglas. How on earth did she get that past her stupid money saving committee? Imagine what that cash could have done for our homeless.

She lowered her voice. 'When they were asked to choose words that best describe me, *harsh, tacky,* and *try-hard* topped the list. Just five per cent said that I speak to cats like them.' Marjorie turned her back to the room and went quiet.

Jitters, sitting all by himself as usual, walked over nervously and gave her a nudge of encouragement. 'It's OK, P-P-P Prime Minister, there was lots of good s-s-stuff in there about you. And you're amongst f-f-friends here.'

'Yes, thank you, Jitters. 31 per cent agreed that I was *hard working*, and a similar number said that I came across as a *strong leader*.'

'A-A-And half of all respondents said th-th-they are p-p-proud that we have Britain's first f-f-female and first moggy Prime Minister.'

'Yes.'

'And when asked what c-c-car you would be, V-V-Volvo came out as the t-t-top answer. I like Volvos, they are s-s-strong and r-r-reliable and —'

'Yes, thanks for that, Jitters,' snapped Marjorie, looking at him threateningly, her eyes widening. The room laughed as he backed away into a corner.

Hector shuddered and let out a yelp. Perhaps he was dreaming about blowing someone up.

'We've all got to work harder,' Marjorie prattled on. 'Less than ten per cent got the name of the Chancellor right, eight in ten have no clue who the, er… Home Secretary is, and the overwhelming majority of those polled say they don't take the Defence Secretary seriously. Frankly, this must change.'

Depends on who's been asked all this, pondered Douglas. *Ordinary cats, those in the slums, they bloody love Hector.*

Speaking of the Defence Secretary, he rose scowling, made his way to the front of the grand room, and jumped up to the window. 'Er, Hector, I'm speaking, in case you didn't realise. Where do you think you are off to?'

'Sorry, Prime Minister, have an appointment. It's kind of important. Doesn't matter anyway, looks like I'm just a common fool, the nation's court jester,' came the sulky reply. The Prime Minister watched on as he eventually climbed through the narrow gap on his fourth attempt, after slipping and making a commotion. The tip of his tail vanished like a flash.

'Back to the results,' Marjorie continued impatiently. 'If they look bad for me, they are a disaster for the leader of the opposition. Some 87 per cent view Kranken as a bit odd, many say his hair is ridiculous, and half the public don't think that cat life and collectivism are compatible.'

'He's just started a podcast, the loon!' shrieked someone at the front hysterically. 'He deserves a good mauling. Live on air!'

Marjorie pounced onto the young MP. 'Rrr-raaow! How dare you talk like that? We don't talk like that on this side!' The black and white cat slipped out of her grasp and scuttled off. 'Have some respect!' growled Marjorie.

The meeting was over. Douglas spotted his opportunity and sidled up to her. He gave her a reassuring nudge. 'Keep your spirits up, Prime Minister, you are strong. And very fashionable, might I add.'

She looked at him with pity in her eyes. No matter, she would be gone soon enough, but for now he would try and get her on side, make her feel good. 'Uh, nice work on the focus groups by the way. Lots to ponder in there, money well spent. Keep fighting the good fight.'

PRESS BRIEFING

Across the city, Hector reclined in the famous *Le Pont* fish restaurant with Angus from *The Meowington Times*. They were hidden in a dimly lit corner. Hector chewed on the mint leaf scooped out of his passionfruit and mint moonshot cocktail. *So, nobody takes me seriously, huh? We'll see about that.*

'Are you OK, Secretary of State? You look agitated.'

'I am most excellent!' he snapped. 'The public will soon see I am not messing around. And once they do, believe me, they... they —'

'OK. But tell me, Hector, you will have heard General Bulgakov's remarks overnight that Britain's days are numbered? What is your response?'

'He'd better watch his back.'

'Care to elaborate?'

'We have spies everywhere, waiting in the shadows, ready to strike at a moment's notice.'

'What, even in Siberia?'

'Yah, everywhere. And we have nukes. And our nukes are bigger than his nukes.'

'Erm, is that the official government line then, Secretary of State?'

'What? I am the flipping government.'

His eyes lit up when his journalist friend offered him some nip leaf. He chewed on it contemplatively, savouring the notes of caramel. 'Look, strictly off the record, you should be turning your attention to the moggy occupying Downing Street.'

'Marjorie Wilson? What about her?'

Hector leaned in. 'Rumour has it that she's got health issues. I have it on good authority that they are pretty serious. That's why she's struggling to do her job. Remember, you didn't hear this from me.'

'Don't worry, I always protect my sources.'

'Fabulous. She is clearly finding it difficult to focus on the job, on the serious existential threats we are facing. The belligerence from that Bulgakov bloke, the mile-long convoy of moggies heading towards us from the Greek Islands. They have almost reached Austria, you know. Alas the Prime Minister is paralysed with her own issues.'

He ordered another passionfruit moonshot. 'If I was a betting tom, I'd say she'd be out within six months.'

'Six months, really?'

'Yahhp! And one more thing, I have it on good authority that her mother was a… a…'

He lowered his voice: 'She was a *stray*. And she fiddled the system to get herself into social housing on a tree estate. You should look into that.'

He peeked over to check Angus was noting everything down.

'Anyway, feel free to take pictures of me while I eat. You have my good side there, Angus.'

'Of course, and would you like copies of these ones too, for your office wall?'

'Yahhp, send me your invoice as usual.'

Hector tucked into his pan-fried sea bass feeling very pleased with himself.

QUESTIONS TO THE PRIME MINISTER!

'Another 10,000 cats homeless and living in bins, just in the last month. It's 'cos this Freedom Cat government is slashing vital benefits. Now, they even wanna take away our most sacred right. To have a decent kip. Has she no shaayme?' Kranken yelled, scowling. His back arched, his hair tied into a top bun.

'Well, look, we are having to take difficult decisions because the Cats Collective ran this country into the ground! Perhaps the Right Honourable Feline would like to, er... well, perhaps he would like to explain to the country what he would do to get us out of his mess?'

Douglas got to his paws and cheered. The leader of the opposition wasn't wrong about the homeless, but he needed to show his support publicly for the PM. She'd be gone soon enough, but for now, it was about getting into her good books. Being the good guy.

'Well, in case she ain't noticed, I weren't running the country back then,' Kranken wailed. 'I would tax the rich and their mansions, give workers a proper wage, protect their sacred right to a decent kip. But I'm the one supposed to be asking the questions, alright?'

There was Ophelia, the so-called Shadow Health Secretary, lying next to him. Nodding gormlessly and giving him licks of encouragement. Irritating and beautiful in equal measures. 'A Freedom Cat government slashing benefits, picking on the poor and vulnerable as usual,' Kranken went on. 'Those on the minimum wage and living in poky cabins in tree estates, suffering once again. Nothing changes with this nasty lot. Has she no shaayme?'

He looked an absolute state with his missing front tooth and his crumpled shirt. 'Fix your stupid hair,' yelled Douglas. 'Have some pride in your appearance!' He felt pleased with that interjection. He'd timed it perfectly.

The Chamber was full. Douglas looked around and observed hundreds of MPs reclining on their red velvet benches, some fast asleep, others nibbling on fried prawn bites fresh out of the Commons Cafeteria. Behind him, two new parliamentarians were scrapping and causing a commotion over a seat.

Marjorie rose. 'Funny that all of us in this House live in mansions, including my Right Honourable Friend. Will he be giving up his mansion any time soon?'

She stared straight at her opponent, her diamond collar sparkling. That Mandy from the bins was right, it was gaudy. She was in her element, though. 'He can shake his head all he wants, it *is* a mansion! And he has the audacity to talk about benefits. The Cats Collective reintroduced benefits into this country, got millions hooked onto, er... well, onto free money! It's how they get their votes. Shame!'

Marjorie let out a hiss. She was in the zone. 'They've learnt nothing from the hooman calamity in our great grandparents' time. Well, this side has. We are cats! Proud! Independent! Agile! And my government will ensure we live like cats once again!'

'You're crackersh, Krank!' slurred Hector, loudly. 'Reducing our great nation to benefits addicts. Criminality at its worsht!'

'Well, lemme put her on notice,' growled the ginger leader of the opposition. 'This side has a conscience. We'll do whatever it takes to block these brutal measures.'

The opposition benches began roaring.

'We will work with anyone,' Kranken continued, 'her teeny, tiny majority ain't gonna be of no use!'

The Defence Secretary looked over. 'Say, Douggy, old chap, are you back in your mansion now?' He was sporting his blue waistcoat, which fitted his podgy Chinchilla body well. It hid most of his ruffled, knotty hair.

'Yes,' whispered Douglas. 'Thanks for asking.'

'Whereabouts is it?' His red eyes were visible through his thick black rimmed glasses.

'Pardon?'

'Your mansion, sir! Where is it?'

'Oh, uh, near, uh… not too far from Victoria. Why do you ask?'

'No reason, just wondered that's all, chap. Say, I'm pleased we aborted our special operation.'

'There was no such thing, Hec,' whispered Douglas. He backed away from the stench of moonshot.

'Listen, we need her out. She is morally weak. I've been taking discreet soundings.'

'Soundings, Hec?'

'Yah, I have at least thirty MPs who would back me if I was to submit a letter of no confidence.'

'Perhaps not the best place to talk about it, Hec, in the middle of PMQs.'

He came closer. 'Don't worry, they're too busy sleeping, stuffing their faces, or fantasising about some wokery or the other. Join me, Douggy. Let's run on a Pahpousson – Schnitty dream ticket. You could be my iron Chancellor?'

'When, Hec?'

'Excellent question! We will need to carry out a very precise operation to remove her. Timing is everything.'

Cor, he'd been busy, thought Douglas. There was no denying that he was a phenomenal orator, and he certainly had a way of connecting with the ordinary cat.

'I'll give it some thought. My only concern right now is to force some emergency funding for the slum cats. In the end, voters will judge us on how we treat the needy.'

'It would be done already if I was in charge.'

Douglas watched his pal as he rolled his nip leaf, trying not to be seen. 'It stinks, Hec.'

'Sorry. You know, Douggy, I blame the Global Cats Alliance for the mess we're in. The wets are holding us back in every aspect of our lives. Economically, militarily, socially, they have turned us into namby-pambys. We should ditch them.'

'I agree, Hec, but she hasn't got the backbone.'

'But perhaps we can use that to our advantage. It could be the very reason we move against her.'

'Go on…'

'Well, this issue of membership can soon reach boiling

point, if we want it to. We have a chance to get in there, create some hoo-hah over this thing. You know, lob in some grenades. She'll want to cling on to the status quo, the battle lines will be drawn, and if we win —'

Douglas closed his eyes. The Global Cats Alliance wasn't all bad. The world's largest union, almost a billion strong, united together, culturally, economically, and socially. It made sense on paper. But it sure sucked with its regulation, its cumbersome bureaucracy, and those stupid pompous politicians poking their snouts into our affairs. 'You're right, Hec. It's high time we left.'

Hector sniffed at the pungent nip leaf. 'Very good. Time to mobilise. If we play this right, we will become the darlings of the Party, the —'

'The saviours of the country. I'll back you, Hec.'

'It's all about getting out of the Global Alliance mentality. Once we are truly free and independent, we can smash this PC generation for good. You and me, Douggy.'

Douglas slumped on his paws for a quick snooze. Some Freedom Cat MP was lecturing the PM on the lack of wind turbines. A loud shriek echoed in the Chamber and made him jump.

'Help! I've been bitten!' It seemed to be coming from the front bench. A scrawny cat had nipped the Chancellor.

'Oh Lord!' screamed Hector. 'We are under attack! From a terrorist!' The little ruffian was weaving in and out of the benches, biting MPs at random. She was shouting something about cruel government policies hurting society, and the need for cats to change their ways. Looked as if she'd been on the nip leaf.

'Think she's from the opposite benches, Hec. Looks like one of the Sharing is Caring lot. They only have two MPs.'

He saw his pal run off and dive into the communal litter tray.

The minister in charge of protecting us, hiding in the toilets.

AN IMPORTANT ANNOUNCEMENT

Douglas hunched over and retched again. Perhaps the fried fish skins he'd shoved down his throat earlier had been dodgy. They had smelt a bit funny come to think of it. He squinted at the screen in his den. The world hunting tournament was showing; England were competing at home, in a forest in Northumberland. We had our lucky red jerseys on. Our side had successfully caught six mice; hunter number 14 scrambled across the line with another furry rodent in between his teeth. He dumped the limp fellow with the pointy snout on the pile, and that made it 7-2 against the German Longhairs. All the sudden movement was hurting Douglas' eyes.

The sound of commentators analysing England's tactics cut off. The screen flickered and flashed to a shot of Number 10 Downing Street. How very strange, he thought. What was she up to now? The cameras started clicking and flashing as the black door opened slightly. Marjorie slipped through the gap and confidently leapt onto the podium, hastily arranging her papers. She was wearing a midnight blue bow on her head and a matching collar.

Hundred per cent CatSaver attire, a couple of British Mews max. That Mandy was on the money, the leader has no class.

'Good evening, or should I say, *hiya*, Prime Minister Marjorie Wilson here. Tonight, I am asking for two minutes of your attention during half time.'

Douglas felt himself dribbling uncontrollably.

'Let me, er… I mean, *lemme* be frank with you.'

Why was she still talking like this? Why?

'I have a big job to do. To balance our, er… well, our books and rescue our economy. We are weeks away from bankruptcy, and sadly, the number of homeless cats living in bins is rising.'

'Stop the cuts then, i-i-idiot,' slurred Douglas. His head was pounding.

'We've had some success already. We have started to cut down on welfare spending. We have saved millions already and we are using these, er… well, these millions on paying down our debts. And as a result, our cost of borrowing, er… well, it is beginning to fall.'

The Prime Minister had a glow in her eyes. She tried to smile; her sharp, pointy teeth on display to the whole country. Oh god, what was she doing?

'We are making progress early in our administration — much like England in tonight's hunt.' She paused awkwardly.

Douglas groaned. He dipped his paw into the puddle of saliva. Surely this wasn't just fried fish skins. Something was wrong.

'But it is not enough,' she jabbered on. 'We need to do more, go deeper. Sadly, the Cats Collective are opposing every policy, every measure, every action. They are against us sleeping less, they are against cutting welfare, they do not want to even have hunting practice in our, er... well, in our nurseries. They are frustrating our recovery, and —'

The Prime Minister stopped in her tracks and looked up at the sky. She squatted on her hind legs and froze. In less than a second, she leapt up and caught a sparrow between her teeth. She gracefully landed back onto the podium playing with her prey as it flapped away between her paws. She looked straight into the camera, taking her eyes off the tiny pale brown bird. He took his chance and flew off unsteadily.

She did that weird smiley thing again. He'd never seen her smile before. Ever. 'They are not, er, I mean, they *ain't* interested in dealing with the difficult challenges that face us. We will not duck these challenges. We will take the tough decisions. It is our job.'

Douglas retched some more. Maybe it was her bizarre smile making him sick.

'And so, I have just chaired a meeting with my Cabinet and we have agreed that the government will call a General Election to take place in, er... well, er...'

'Oh, fuck,' said Douglas.

'In, er, six weeks' time. I ask you to give me a decent majority so I can fix the economy and bring you prosperity. Thank you. Oh, and come on In-ger-land!' She was beaming.

'Oh, fuck,' said Douglas over and over. He collapsed onto his side twitching sharply. Funny that the tiger lily had disappeared after the Black Cats Society meeting. That bastard Hector must have swiped it.

He dialled the emergency vet. 'Hello, Douglas Schnitty here, help me please,' he slurred. 'I've been poisoned.'

OUR GLORIOUS GARDEN

A speech by Hector Perp Pahpousson.

[THANK HOST. GIVE HER A LICK ON CHOPS.]

Our countryside must be protected like a delicate newborn Holly Blue or Lulworth Skipper.

I'd like to thank the Countryside Society, a very fine organisation, for inviting me to speak at your 100th anniversary. If this were to be my final dinner before I depart this life, every single one of you would be guest of honour! And we would drink the finest moonshot money could buy!

We have a joint mission. We stand shoulder to shoulder with a special ambition in common. A burning desire to protect our countryside for we are lucky to live together in one big, glorious garden.

And so, we have won the lottery of life along with our elegant language, our hunting prowess, our cuisine, culture, sartorial eloquence… I digress.

[BRING ATTENTION TO SOPHISTICATED NECKWEAR. MOST SUBTLY.]

Tonight, we are here to talk about our glorious national garden. It must be cherished. We must stand up for our glorious garden; speak up for our glorious garden; and protect our glorious garden.

We must grow in abundance the queen of British trees, the Beech, and the Hawthorn, the Willow and the Sycamore. We must grow in abundance the Holly Tree, planted back in the day as a protection from witches.

[REMOVE SPECTACLES TO DEMONSTRATE GRAVITAS.]

Let's protect our trees, and I speak not of the hooman inspired, rough and raggedy estates, of which we have more than enough. We must not sabotage our glorious garden, we must not sacrifice our green beauty and natural diversity for the ugly demands of modern life. The last lot did that much too often in the name of "collectivism".

Let's instead build homes for our dormouse cousins, and the nightingale. The playful badger, the resourceful vole, and the beautifully elusive bat. The great otters and beavers and nimble deer.

Yes, we may want to hunt them down, pounce on them, and sink our claws into them — but we must resist the urge, for they too are part of our society.

Our future must be one of peace, serenity, and calm. I want my kittens, and my kittens' kittens, to be able to run in golden fields of wheat freely without reprimand or retribution.

I want them to be able to coexist peacefully with the dormouse, without gobbling it up for tea.

And so, we must be bold, we must be shameless, and we must be reckless in protecting our beautiful countryside.

Otherwise our efforts will be flocci; our efforts will be nauci; our efforts will be nihili; our efforts will be pilifi.

[SLOW DOWN FOR EFFECT.]

Indeed my friends, our efforts will be floccinaucinihil-ipilification.

Thank you.

[REMAIN STILL AND SOAK UP OVATION. NOD AT SOCIETY PRESIDENT.]

ACT TWO

MEMO ON
MP OFFICES

Douglas was back to feeling his usual self. He'd been in to see the vet, who told him in no uncertain terms that he'd suffered from a bout of food poisoning, and nothing more. He'd been given a stern lecture on watching what he puts inside him. 'If the fish skins smell rotten, they most probably are rotten,' the vet had said, looking unimpressed. 'You really shouldn't be eating them in the first place.'

He clicked on an email titled *MEMO ON MP OFFICES*.

Dear Colleague,

As you are aware, my government is working hard to bring our public expenditure down so we can pay off our debts and once again live within our means.

You will be aware that I had recently instructed my Emergency Money Saving Committee to look into the potential cost savings from vacating our hundreds of MP office spaces across the country. I have since received and carefully scrutinised the findings, and I can tell you that we will save more than half a million British Mews every year if this measure is implemented.

Time is of the essence; we are throwing away thousands in rent every single day. You are therefore required to vacate your office space within five days — unless you are a government minister, in which case you are exempt from this order.

Of course, as a politician you will have your mansion which you can work from, and I would encourage you to do this. I would also urge you to spend more time out and about amongst the communities you serve.

Thank you for your understanding. You are playing a fundamental part in rescuing our country from bankruptcy.

Yours,

Prime Minister Marjorie Wilson.

Douglas clawed the memo to shreds. The nerve to lecture us about spending more time in the communities we serve — she wouldn't even meet Mandy. And what the hell was he supposed to do with Shuffles? Where were they supposed to go now? Where would he keep their things? All her food? She was having a snooze, blissfully unaware. He curled up into a ball.

A PROPER WAGE

Jitters was drooling over the stuffed mice and fattened pigeon hanging inside the window of his favourite deli. It was thriving since it opened last year, and he felt lucky to have it on his doorstep. He, along with about fifty others, was trying to get to the counter to order some breakfast. A half-orderly queue had quickly disintegrated into mayhem.

He saw a familiar looking figure ahead of him causing a commotion and holding everyone up. He recognised that top bun anywhere. It was that Kranken, the leader of the opposition, and he appeared to be having a barney with Pierre, the deli owner.

'For the love of God, can we just start the damn podcast?'

'But 30 British Mews an hour?' Pierre scoffed. 'That is just crazy. I would have to put up the price of this latte fivefold at least. Forget about it.'

'I'm telling you, it's the right thing to do. Over many decades, the Freedom Cats have allowed poverty to rise and rise, and millions have been forgotten. It's sickening. We can't carry on just thinking of ourselves —'

'I have to serve my customers soon, monsieur —'

'OK, this won't take long. Welcome to the Krankcast —'

'No, sorry, stop recording. I just don't agree with this,' said Pierre, abruptly.

'But why? Wouldn't it be a beautiful world if we changed our ways and stopped being so damn individualistic? A compulsory minimum wage, set in the region of 30 British Mews, would be a good start.'

'Mais I proudly pay my workers 10 British Mews an hour,' said Pierre. 'Being forced to almost triple this is madness. I would have to put up my prices, perhaps you would like to pay three times more for your milky latte?'

'I'm sure that won't be necessary, Pierre.'

Well, this was quite the turn out for the books, thought Jitters. He edged closer to the ruckus and hit the big red button on his phone.

'Look at the bigger picture, will you?' Kranken continued. 'We'll be putting cash into the pockets of those that really need it.'

'I-I would love to pay my workers more, bien sur, mais where do you expect small b-businesses like me to find the money from?' stuttered Pierre. 'At least say you will exempt small businesses from this?'

Jitters checked his screen. The little red soundwave lines were zigzagging up and down, doing their thing.

'Exemptions become tricky, they create grey areas, and those at the top will always try and play the system,' Kranken whined. 'Put it this way, your workers will be better off, they'll be able to afford to put food in their bowls, and pay their rent. They'll be happier as a result. Now, welcome to the Krankcast —'

'Rrr-aaow! Get out!' screeched Pierre, baring his sharp teeth.

'But they deserve a proper wage they can live on,' whimpered Kranken, slowly backing off.

'Just leave. And take your milky latte with you. L'idiot.'

'But what about my podcast?'

Jitters hit the stop button and uploaded the recording onto his email. This was top notch material, the boss would be very pleased. Kranken also lived in the neighbourhood. *He'd better be careful*, mused Jitters. *They won't appreciate his funny collectivism thing around these parts.*

MOVING IN DAY.
AGAIN

Douglas' new home stank of rotten eggs and piss. Still, at least it was his own space. He unknotted the bits of string holding his casework files together and tied them to the four bins he'd hastily arranged in an oblong-like shape. The string would act as his walls for now, his fortress. He threw his shirts on them. The shirts would give him some privacy. The shirts that were freshly washed in the river. The shirts that would now have the scent of rotten eggs seeped into them.

There was a debate kicking off down the way. 'I'd feel much safer out here if I had a gun, that's all I'm saying,' said someone.

'That's crazy,' said another. 'All them lootings we're seeing would turn into shootings, innit.'

'But at least we would be able to defend our families like our Maine Coon cousins,' replied the first.

Douglas crouched down, best not to attract attention. He shoved Shuffles' food and his precious nip leaf parcels into a tatty cardboard box that he'd bagsied. It would all stay dry in there at least. He looked through the nest of leaves he'd made for her. She peered right back at him through her bottle.

'Sorry you've been downsized, little one. It's just temporary. I'll fix this for us, I promise.' He arranged the leaves over her bottle. 'Good night, Shuffles, you'll be safe under there.'

He opened his correspondence file. The priority cases were building up thick and fast. Tomorrow he'd hold his nose and pay the Prime Minister a visit; she'd finally agreed to a meeting and had invited him for drinks in Downing Street. The change of strategy, the flattery, seemed to be working on her. But for now, it was time to get to work.

Dear Douglas Schnitty,

I've been waiting for a cabin in the trees for well over four months now. The council are useless, they've stopped responding to me. I'm not very good at hunting and there are only so many flies one can eat. The bins are bad, the noise and antisocial behaviour is affecting my mental health. Please can you see what you can do?

Fran, SW1

He looked up and saw an elderly she-cat staring at him. She was garbling away to herself, licking the fur on her back frantically.

BLACK OPS

Hector was drunkenly purring with about eighty or so colleagues in the lair of the Black Cats Society. They had spent the last hour grumbling about their moggy Prime Minister. He had listened intently to a theory that she had been bought off by the Cats Collective. She was deliberately performing badly, explained a voice in the shadows, and she had come to some sort of arrangement to get the leader of the opposition into power. Sounded credible, he thought. There existed no smoke without fire. They had voted overwhelmingly in favour of putting both her and Kranken, under 24/7 surveillance. A permanent black ops unit would be set up immediately.

He'd been doing the rounds earlier, topping up bowls with his precious moonshot, gifting various colleagues pots of cream, hinting most subtly about his strong leadership credentials. Everyone was clamouring to be his Chancellor for some reason. He hadn't promised a thing, or at least he didn't think he had. His mind was fuzzy on the specifics. He closed his eyes and ran through his lines. This was his big chance.

Mukerjee, the Society elder, made his way to the stage, limping on a wooden stick. Rumour had it he had got into a late-night scrap with someone in the Speaker's office inside

Parliament. All over who got dibs on a stray mouse in the corridor, and it had got nasty.

'Next item on the agenda, the membershiiiip of the Global Cats Alliaaaance,' he bellowed.

'Good luck, buddy,' whispered his pal, Douglas. He smelt like a bog.

Hector rose and licked his lips. He'd taken a last-minute swig of the smooth moonshot for luck. It embraced his tongue much like his silk pyjamas embraced him. He glanced around for a full minute, making eye contact with those awake. He cleared his throat. 'Our dear moggy leader has only gone and called a snap election. Promising an assortment of measly cuts won't help us win it.'

'Damn right,' shouted someone.

'We need to think bigger,' the Defence Secretary continued. 'We need to consider how we can fix our monumental problems; an imminent attack from Bulgakov, our starved army, cats in the bins.'

They were listening avidly.

'I say it's high time we left the over-bearing and bureaucratic Global Cats Alliance.'

The lair erupted in a cheer and celebration.

'Those that run it are nothing more than a bunch of self-important lollygaggers in cheap suits,' he chimed. 'We need to free ourselves and take back control! Take back control of our money! Our laws! And our borders!'

He peeked around, feeling pleased with himself. 'We can make the election about the Global Alliance if we are clever.'

Someone offered him a swig of moonshot. 'Why, thank you, don't mind if I do. Er, and once we say "hasta la vista, baby" to those cheap-suited bureaucrats, we can build a beautiful wall. Keep out those damn immigrants… I mean —'

'OK, time's up!' Mukerjee cut him off. 'Vote in favour of leaving the Global Cats Alliance say aye!'

'Aaaaaaaaye!' roared the room.

'Vote against leaving the Global Cats Alliance say nay.'

'Naaaay!' echoed a solo high-pitched voice from the back of the lair.

Hector darted clumsily to the back of the room to try and locate the objector. It didn't matter. The highly influential Black Cats Society had voted to back him, and leave the Global Cats Alliance by 77-1.

BE STRONG,
PRIME MINISTER.

Douglas sat in the corner of the Downing Street study. Having a roof over his head was not to be sniffed at these days. He had passed that Jitters downstairs, sprawled out, snoring away. What the hell was the Minister for Welfare and General Sums doing here at this time? He had to step over his podgy midriff to get past, he was completely out of it. Oh well, it was none of his business.

He observed the Prime Minister as she supped on her fruity moonshot. Supping away in her magnificent office. Her magnificently unnecessary office. Maybe she should lead by example and vacate it.

'I had to call the election, Douglas. The, er... public finances are in a seriously bad way.'

He prowled towards the open fire, wincing at her garish red and gold décor.

'And I won't be able to get any of my money saving measures through Parliament with Kranken's lot,' she droned on. 'They keep blocking every solution we come up with, and they have no alternative. We need a, er... well, a bigger majority; I had no choice.'

Her red and gold décor was even more extreme than her cuts. It didn't matter, they would be the end of her very soon. For now, "operation good guy" was in full swing. 'Don't worry, Prime Minister, you are doing the right thing. We will only fix the economy with the right medicine, and it needs to be the strong stuff.'

He paused and peeked over at her. 'We mustn't waver; our kittens, and their kittens, will never forgive us.'

'See, you understand. It is my duty to ensure I, er… well, I do the right thing. But have you seen the furore? The scenes on the news look bad, Douglas, the shops in London and Manchester have been vandalised and looted. There is anger out there.'

The manure-like stench of the leather on her sofas made him feel sick. It was worse than the bloody bins. Having a PM who couldn't care less about the slum cats made him feel even sicker. He had tried, really tried. He attempted to spell out the merits of a dedicated minister for the homeless, and the desperate need for emergency aid. He had broached it at least six times, in the simplest of English, and she just gawped with a blank expression each time. Rabbiting on about the necessity of a slimmed down government and fiscal discipline. The same old tired lines. She hadn't listened to a word he said.

'Be strong, Prime Minister. You must come down hard on the perpetrators. And keep going with the cuts, in fact you must go further. Show some steel.'

'Yes, I will be ordering a curfew from tomorrow…'

'Good,' said Douglas. The harsher her actions, the bigger the revolt, he thought. The quicker her demise.

'Uh, get the troops and water cannon on standby too,' he continued. 'Show them you mean business. Remember your 69 focus groups, the public see you as a strong leader. Times like this call for strong leadership.'

She poured herself another moonshot. 'And as for that bloody Hector, why has he started up about leaving the Global Cats Alliance? I make him Defence Secretary, and this is how he repays me?'

'Ah, yes, Hector —'

'He's caused me no end of problems; so many on our side want out, the President of the Alliance has now got wind of it and wants, er… well, he wants an urgent meeting.'

'The pressure is mounting, isn't it, Prime Minister?' Douglas went and lay next to her. 'Don't worry about Hector.'

'I don't care about Hector, it's the Black Cats Society I worry about,' said Marjorie. 'Once they get their claws into something, there's no stopping them. You seem, er… well, you seem well connected with that lot?'

'Uh, not really. I, uh, mainly observe from the side lines,' said Douglas.

'Well, maybe you can have a word? Just tell them to, er… well, to back off a bit. Until after the election at least.'

'I'll see what I can do. But it may not be such a bad idea to confront this thorny issue once and for all. Imagine if you are the one who fixes it. Imagine if we can use the millions saved from membership of the Global Alliance to make slums history.'

His heart fluttered in a moment of excitement. 'Think of your legacy, Prime Minister!'

'It's impossible right now, Douglas. I would use the money to, er… well, to pay down our debts.'

He felt the urge to bite her. It was time to get out of there before he did something he regretted.

'Go meet the President, anyway,' he said.

'I'll sleep on it.'

'I'll come with you. I'll look after you, Prime Minister.'

ANOTHER ROLLOCKING

In Whitehall, Hector was busy googling his name.

'Hec-toor! Where are you? Hec-toor! You have no idea how livid I am!'

The black Chinchilla twitched nervously, racking his brains. *What's bothering her now?*

'Where is he? Someone must have seen him,' demanded Fee, prowling up and down the corridor. 'I can smell his fish which he obviously stuck in the bloody microwave. AGAIN! Hector! I know you're here because I can smell your bloody fish which you've once again put in the microwave! It stinks!'

'It stinks,' mimicked Hector, under his breath.

He composed himself. She was never happy. So bloody sensitive, so PC. So easily offended. She wouldn't have lasted five minutes in the army.

'I quote, "Our nukes are bigger than his nukes," really, Hector? Are you going out of your way to start a war?'

He breathed softly, staying as still as possible. Why did he have to work with such a snowflake? The only thing Bulgakov would understand is strength, it was plainly obvious.

He eyed up the slightly ajar window above him.

'Hector – come out from wherever you're hiding. We need to talk urgently. Number 10 keep calling. They reckon they've got wind of you hatching something concerning the Global Cats Alliance. They are seething!'

He could hear Fee darting around, getting closer.

'And they're convinced you've been spreading rumours about the Prime Minister's mother. Is that true, Hector?'

He could hear her sniffing with determination. 'They're mad at you because you keep poking your nose into other ministers' briefs. They want to see you… you could be sacked tonight.'

Hoy! He leapt up clumsily onto the window ledge and hoisted himself through the tiny gap.

RANSOM NOTE

'You need to get yourself lower, much lower,' said Douglas. The black kitten was doing well.

'Crouch down and stay there. Literally freeze yourself in that position.'

The ginger one's legs were trembling under the strain.

'Try and relax, you need to stay like that for as long as it takes. Patience is the name of the game. And the more you practice, the stronger those leg muscles will get.'

Douglas paced up and down. It was a hot day, and the neighbourhood was smelling especially rancid. 'Now, remember the element of surprise. Camouflage whenever you can, be creative. You need to be able to see them at all times. They must never see you. If your prey spots you, it's game over.'

It was disgusting that hunting was banned from schools under the last government. Youngsters had missed out on essential survival skills for a decade, they may as well have become hoomans.

'Bend your legs and pounce! Go! That's good… and again!'

If he were in charge, every homeless cat would receive hunting lessons free of charge. They wouldn't go hungry ever again.

'Good! And I want to see you use those claws. And those gnashers! God gave them to you for a reason.'

The black and ginger kittens were excitedly clawing and biting the air. Watching them was an uplifting experience, their zest was joyful. Douglas felt immense pride in teaching the next generation such vital skills.

'Good, well done. Keep practising, and you will soon be able to provide for your families. Tomorrow we will hunt for real.'

'Do we get to eat our prey, sir?' asked the ginger one.

'Of course! But you have to catch it first.'

'Yessir,' they chimed in unison.

'And never forget the element of surprise. You have got to outwit your prey, do the unexpected. They expect you to go left, so you must dart to the right. It's an instinct.'

'Yessir. Thank you, sir.'

'My pleasure, kitties, now who would like to take on an important job?'

'Me! Me!'

Douglas shoved about 100 sealed envelopes and packages their way. 'OK, you can both do it. Deliver these to my constituents, please read their names and addresses carefully, OK? It's important they get the right letters.'

It was time for some shuteye; training the youth had taken it out of him. And Shuffles could probably do with a snack too. Douglas trotted onto his patch, dodging his hanging laundry. Leaves were scattered everywhere.

'Shuffles?'

His friend was nowhere to be seen. Douglas rummaged inside the cardboard box.

'Shuffles?' She wasn't amongst his files. He patted the rug, it was all dusty and gross.

'Ha-choo! Oh God, Shuffles? Where have you gone?'

He spotted an envelope propped up against one of the bins. His name was scrawled on the front.

Douglas Schnitty,

We know who you are. You earn mega bucks as a politician, so what business do you have living here? We have your precious fish, you weirdo. She is safe. Five grand and we will return her alive. Await further instructions.

'Shuffles? Shuffles! Dear God, no! Please! Whoever you are, please bring her back! She's all I've got. Shuffles!'

Not a peep from anyone. The crazy she-cat neighbour was staring with her wide eyes, moving her head madly.

THE BATTLE BUS

Hector was in the Commons Cafeteria. He'd been sitting by the window and staring out of it for a solid three hours. He felt relieved, and a little proud of himself, to have dodged that mad Fee. With such skill.

His tail was gently brushing the floor from side to side. He didn't want to be disturbed. The wets at Number 10 could say what they like, it wouldn't stop him on his quest to free the country from the crooks at the Global Alliance. He wanted to urgently get his paws on a battle bus, but first he had to find some donors to fund it. He took out his fountain pen.

Let's break free from the shackles.
Ditch the Global Alliance!

He scribbled it out. The bus needed a catchy slogan. Something in big letters that resonated all over the country. Something like: *Slash the bureaucracy!* Or *Make Britain Strong Again!*

'Hello, Hector, got a minute?'

'Hello, hi, hi.'

'I've given your proposal some consideration and I would be delighted to serve as your Chancellor, should you end up going for it.'

'What's that?'

'Remember we talked about my Chancellorship in your administration?'

'Er, fabulous,' muttered the Defence Secretary. He had no idea who the bloke was, presumably one of the Black Cats Society from the other night. 'Yahhp, fabulous. Let's stay in touch, yah? And keep it hush hush for the time being.'

What the hell had happened the other night? Who on earth was he? A spotted woodpecker caught his eye as it hopped about on the blossoming cherry tree outside. It was making him rather peckish.

He took a swig from his hipflask. The tonic would aid the mental arithmetic. *We're sending 300 millon British Mews a year to the Global Alliance. That's about 4.5 billion over an average lifetime...*

'Greetings, H-H-Hector, how's it g-g-g-going?' came another, rather nervous-sounding, voice from behind.

He ignored it. Probably best not to make any more promises.

'H-H-H-Hector? Hello?'

Hector's eyes remained firmly fixed on the woodpecker.

In our lifetime on this earth, we will have forked out 4.5 billion British Mews to the Global Alliance. We could give that to the military instead. Yes, that would resonate. But not enough sass...

Ah, the wall of course! Hector leapt up onto a nearby table, knocking water onto a well-dressed she-cat he didn't recognise.

'Stop giving money to the crooked Global Alliance,' he announced. 'Let's instead give it to our military, and wait for it... build a wall! A big, beautiful wall! Keep out the immigrants, I mean the illegals!' he shrieked. 'That, my friends, will keep us safe.'

The cafeteria looked on, in stunned silence. The she-cat was giving him daggers, her blouse drenched. He murmured an apology and shuffled off.

He would welcome his fellow country cats onto his battle bus, rally the masses. Perhaps he would drive it to Downing Street and block the entrance until the glorious leader succumbed. She would have no choice but to put the issue at the forefront of the election manifesto. But there was one dear friend he needed to consult, and get on board, if this was to succeed. He understood this cat well. He liked him.

Hector whipped out his phone and began typing.

> Let us rendezvous tomorrow, 10pm. At the secret treetop. We need to talk. Bring your finest liquor. And not a word to anyone. Lots of love.

*

'Wow, how much did that cost?' asked the ginger kitten rubbing himself against Douglas' watch.

'Uh, not too sure. But look, I can take pictures on it.'

'Cool!'

'And look, it tells me how many steps I've done.'

'Wow! I wish I had one.'

Douglas' eyes were drooping. He'd been awake for nine hours straight looking for his little orange friend. He'd clocked up 5,750 steps around the slum, making enquiries from patch to patch, bin to bin. Not a single lead. He'd managed to respond to dozens more constituents in between his enquiries.

'Listen, would you like another job, little one?'

'Yessir! I would!'

Douglas put a small satchel over the kitten's neck. 'OK, take the parcels inside to the names and addresses written on them. Don't lose them whatever you do. And bring me back the envelopes you are given.'

'Yessir. What's in the parcels?'

'Oh, just, uh, some medicine. Do not show anyone. And this package addressed to Maples is very important. Deliver that one first.'

'Yessir.'

And when you return, we can do some more hunting practice. Deal?'

'Deal!'

'Don't forget to bring me back the envelopes, and do not lose them.' Douglas lay his head down. Everyone was keeping shtum about Shuffles. He'd find the five grand if he had to. He heard a scratch on one of the bins. 'Psst, are you Douglas Schnitty? I have something for you.'

Douglas saw a ginger and white paw push a glass object through his hanging shirts. There was a bright thing bobbing around inside.

'Oh my God! Sh-Shuff... No!'

'Keep your voice down, mate.'

There she was prancing about excitedly in her cosy bottle.

'Oh, thank God! Where was she?'

'One of the gangs across the way, mate. They had her.'

'Jeez, thanks! Who are you? I must repay you.'

'Nah, don't worry, mate. You taught my little one how to hunt. I'm really grateful. You're a good guy.'

'It's no problem —'

'But you gotta listen to me. You're not safe around here, and neither is she. Word has got round about who you are. You should leave while you can. Them lot will keep going after you.'

'Thanks for the heads up, uh, why don't you come in? There must be something I can do, some way I can, uh...'

The visitor pitter-pattered off into the night.

LIFE COACHES
FOR THE NATION.

Douglas was whisked out of the snug and warm limousine, into the London Broadcasting Studios.

He was pleased that the Prime Minister had asked him to appear on *Talk to Bromfield*, the leading midnight talk show in the country. She'd mentioned something on the phone about reconsidering how the membership money would be allocated if they left the Global Alliance. 'Douglas, we must absolutely pay down our debts,' she lectured at him. And then she went on to talk about looking at "other national priorities"; she had referred to them as the "forgotten priorities". Said she thought there could be a spare 50 million in the first year of leaving the Alliance which could be committed to these priorities. Her Emergency Money Saving Committee was considering it apparently. It was all a bit vague, but a huge step in the right direction. She'd promised him another meeting "within days".

He was beginning to get through to her; and she was putting her trust in him. The plan was working. He had just found out that he was going to be pitted against the crazy

Ophelia. She had a habit of shouting and talking over her opponents; it was probably for the best that he handled this one.

He caught her eye as he entered the studio and gave her a polite meow. He noticed her beautifully painted pink claws. She hissed back at him. Typical.

'Tonight, we are joined by senior Freedom Cat Douglas Schnitty and Shadow Health Secretary Ophelia Peaches. And what looks like a fish?'

'Uh, yes, this is Shuffles. Hope you don't mind her tagging along?'

'Well, luckily for her, I've just eaten. Welcome onto the programme.' Mrs Bromfield spoke in her usual low pitched and slightly irritated manner. Her show had been going strong for five years.

'Ophelia, let's begin with you. We have an election around the corner, what are the Cats Collective offering?'

'Well, I can announce exclusively on your programme tonight… 50,000 life coaches for the nation.'

'Pardon?'

'We promise 50,000 life coaches for the nation, if we win the election.'

'Er, OK, what exactly will they do, Shadow Minister?'

'Well, they will, um… they will make the nation happier and healthier. They will send a message in the strongest terms that we can all be who we want to be, no matter where we come from.'

'And how much will this policy cost, Ophelia?'

'Trust you to get straight onto the figures,' hissed the Shadow Health Secretary.

'Well, they are important,' said Mrs Bromfield, 'especially now, when we are near bankrupt as a country.'

'Yes, they are important,' echoed Douglas. He winked at Shuffles.

'Oh, do shut up, Douglas,' growled Ophelia. 'You stink of garbage by the way. Look, we're looking at recruiting 50,000 life coaches and we're confident we can do this easily for five million.'

'Five million? British Mews?' asked Mrs Bromfield.

'Ears.'

'Pardon?'

'Ears.'

'Uh, I think she's saying yes, in her hoity-toity manner,' mumbled Douglas.

'Do please shut up, Douglas. Protecting our public finances will always come first with the Cats Collective.'

'Quiet please, Douglas, we will come to you in a minute,' snapped Mrs Bromfield. 'For how long? How long a period does the five million cover?'

'A year of course,' replied Ophelia, 'and that's fantastic value if you think about it. Five million may sound like a lot, but imagine if that money can make a nation happier, healthier, and more equal.'

'Er, that's 100 British Mews per life coach, Shadow Minister. 100 British Mews for the whole year. Will that just go towards their expenses, then? Will they be volunteers?'

'No, of course not,' snapped Ophelia. 'Life coaches need to live too, and they need a fair wage especially when they will be working round the clock to fix our nation's health. They will not live in poverty, on zero hours contracts.'

'OK, but your five million estimate works out at 100 British Mews each…'

'Um, er, no, I don't think it does.'

'I can assure you it does,' said Mrs Bromfield, her eyes narrowing.

'Er… er… shoot. I mean 50 million. Yes, 50 million British Mews. Sorry I have not yet had my evening nip leaf.'

'And how much does that work out to per life coach?'

'I beg your pardon?'

'50 million for 50,000 life coaches – how much is that per life coach, Shadow Minister?'

'One million British Mews, of course. But don't forget the immense value they will bring to the nation. Without them —'

'Wait, you're saying that your life coaches will get paid a million per year?'

'Yes,' replied Ophelia, but we need to get away from our obsession of a low wage —'

'Sorry to talk over you but that is a rather incredible amount of money and —'

'Yes, but compared to what? How much are the top England hunters in the World Hunting Tournament earning?'

'Ophelia — not only is this a barmy amount, but it's still wrong!'

'I beg your pardon?'

'50 million divided by 50,000 is not a million. It's a thousand. You're going to pay your coaches 1,000 British Mews per year?'

'Um… yes, but look, why are you so obsessed with the numbers? We're not even in power yet so we have time to get the figures right. If we tax our citizens properly and fairly, we can afford this very nice policy. For the nation.'

'You're making it up as you go along.'

'Rubbish!' hissed Ophelia. 'This country is too obsessed with the numbers. The Freedom Cats know the price of everything but the value of nothing.'

Douglas reclined underneath the microphone and closed his eyes. It was nice and snug in the studio and he was feeling rather pleased about how it was going. The Cats Collective were a joke. The best thing he could do right now was to lay low. Let Ophelia keep talking, keep digging.

'So, your life coaches will be paid 1,000 British Mews per year. But you still want to introduce a 30 British Mews per hour compulsory minimum wage?'

'Yes, it will go a great way towards bringing equality and ending discrimination.'

'Well, how much will it cost to you to pay your 50,000 life coaches this compulsory minimum wage?' Mrs Bromfield looked like she was about to pounce.

'So roughly in the region of about…' Ophelia broke out into a coughing fit. It looked like she was bringing up a hairball.

'I have an abacus if you'd like to borrow it, Shadow Health Secretary,' whispered Douglas into the microphone, sniggering.

'Alright, Douglas, let's come to you. At least the Cats Collective are offering us something positive, what are you offering us?'

'Well, firstly I'd like to say what a pleasure it is to be here with you tonight. Your programme is fantastic, I am a huge fan.'

He paused and slow blinked at Mrs Bromfield. She scowled back.

'It's no wonder you are soaring in the ratings,' he continued in his best radio voice.

'What are you offering us, Douglas?'

'Now then, we are the ones clearing up the mess left by her Party, and unfortunately that means taking some very difficult decisions.'

'Isn't it true that your Party has nothing positive to offer the country?'

'On the contrary Mrs Bromfield, you will see that our Prime Minister is performing the rather delicate balancing act of cutting our debt, slashing our taxes, and helping create jobs and opportunities.'

'Yes, and talking away our right to sleep. Speaking of the Prime Minister, the public find her a bit tacky, a bit fake, don't they? Do you?'

'Look, it's not about what I think, Mrs Bromfield. What I can tell you is that Marjorie is the right cat for the job. For now.'

'For now, huh? Well, thank you both, that's all we have time for.'

Ophelia jabbed her claws into Douglas' tail and ran out. He squealed.

'Ophelia, what the hell was that?' boomed a familiar gravelly voice outside the studio. It was Kranken.

'Oh, hi there, Leader, I know! Did you hear the bias in that interview?'

'Ophelia — it was a bloody car crash! I told you to dial down the life coach chat, it comes across as weird!'

'I wouldn't worry, Leader, I exposed the scummy media for what it is.'

'No, you came off worse for wear against a third-rate Freedom Cat! And you showed the country that you can't do simple mathematics.'

'I think we need to add Mrs Bromfield to our media boycott list,' declared Ophelia, following Kranken down the corridor.

'Everyone knows she is a biased, bitter old hag,' she continued. 'Her mother was a Freedom Cat MP, you know.'

'Yes, I am aware of that!'

'I say no more interviews on her show! I am feeling optimistic if you ask me. Life coaches for the country is a winning policy, ears.'

Douglas cackled as Ophelia's voice trailed off in the distance. He winced at the stabbing pain in his tail, and then cackled some more. Five weeks until the election and that interview could not have gone better. The PM was bound to be happy with it too. He needed her to start seeing him as dependable, a steady performer. That interview would have done the job.

*

Three days since the interview and nothing from the PM. Not even a "thanks" or a "good job".

Dear Prime Minister,

I trust you were happy with my showing on Mrs Bromfield's show the other night? If Ophelia Peaches is the best they can put up in the run up to an election, then we have nothing to worry about. You'd mentioned a follow-up meeting within days to discuss our forgotten national priorities, when suits you?

Warm wishes,

The Rt Hon Douglas Schnitty

THE SECRET TREETOP MEETING

Douglas zigzagged through the muddy woodland at Newlands Corner. Still nothing from the PM; it was just bad manners. He would hear out the Defence Secretary, see what he had to say. He stopped casually at the foot of the sweeping willow tree, glanced around, and waded through the leaves. He was confident he hadn't been followed. He climbed with care.

'Pssst, over here, chum,' came a whisper from above. Douglas glanced up and spotted a bushy black tail swinging like a pendulum. It was a grey and overcast afternoon and Douglas' fur was wet from the drizzle. They bumped heads lightly in greeting.

'Wah! I spy a little bottle in the satchel, exciting!'

'Not what you think, Hec, sorry.'

'Golly, is something moving in there or am I hallucinating again?'

'It's, uh, my friend. Shuffles. Hope you don't mind her tagging along.'

Hector's nostrils went into overdrive. 'Is she a fish?'

'Yes.'

'Ooh, a little shnack? Exciting!'

'No! Not a snack! Look, Hec, don't worry about her. You won't even know she's here.'

'Righty-ho. Well, try this, old chap,' said Hector, revealing a bottle in a regal looking red box. 'Japanese. Oodles of fruit and spice. Matured for 10 years.'

'Ooh, how novel,' remarked Douglas.

'Now then, work with me on the Global Alliance campaign. You and I can lead this thing.'

Douglas sampled the moonshot.

'Furthermore, I've got almost 50 names.'

'For what, Hec?'

'50 MPs that have pledged allegiance to me if I make a move, they've signed up to serve in my government. I've even bought the hot for Hec web domain.'

'Uh, hot for Hec?'

'Yahhp! You know, www dot hot for me, Hec, dot com. 50 MPs are hot for me so far. Bloody marvellous.'

Crackers, thought Douglas. But imagine the good he could do with that kind of popularity.

He slurred on. 'We'd have the biggest army in the world under my shtewardship, I will take out that Bulgakov myself.'

A bit mad, but maybe he'd be worth the risk.

'Would you come and meet my poor constituents living in the bins, Hec?'

'I would be their very best friend, sir!' The Defence Secretary supped away at the Japanese moonshot.

'That's good, but what they really need is package of financial assistance to get them —'

'Done! My government will put our troops and our homeless first!'

Douglas' ears pricked up. 'OK, well, that's exciting, Hec, but where will we find the dosh?'

'What?'

'The financial assistance will cost at least —'

'Let's worry about the finer detail later. We will find a way through the workings of our superior minds.' He tipped the bowl over his head, drenching himself.

Seemed like the bowl of moonshot talking again, making empty promises.

'OK, Hec, but going back to the homeless for a sec —'

'Yahhp, yahhp, don't worry about it. Trust old Hec.'

On the flip side, what if he ended up being a worse PM than Marjorie? At least she's sane, he could get us annihilated.

Hector continued, 'For now, we need to get the masses riled up. You know, we need a bloody big bus to drive up and down the country.'

Oh, here we go. The bus again...

'And we need a bloody big slogan on it. Big bold letters plastered all over the side of the thing.'

'What would it say, Hec?'

Hector's nose started to twitch in excitement. 'Ditch the bastards! The useless, tubby suits at the top of the Alliance. Time to pull our tanks out of there!'

Douglas felt a surge of energy. Moonshot-fuelled energy. He swigged the remainder back.

'Make Britain great again!' continued his friend. 'That sort of thing. In caps!'

'Ooh yes, I like that.' Douglas slowly flicked the tip of his tail in thought. 'You know, Hec, the public will adore someone who talks straight.'

'Yahhp, we must be bombastic in our quest. The very opposite of the kind of bland suits that surround the Prime Minister. Useless lot.'

'Yes, quite.'

'Shmucks!'

'Indeed.'

Hector topped up his moonshot. 'What if we were to promise every household some sort of dividend from all the money we save?'

Douglas covered his eyes. 'Hector Perp Pahpousson, I can't believe what a genius you are!'

'Thank you. You know, I did some simple mathematics, Douglas, and worked out that we spend something like 4.5 billion British Mews on membership in our lifetime. That equates to —'

'Yes, yes, very good, Hec, but go easy on the detail. The public won't want to be put through a maths exam. You need to give it to them straight, say the things that others are too afraid to.'

'Yes! I knew this project belonged to us! They can go whistle for their money!' shouted Hector. 'Our money! Our freedom! Our sovereignty!'

'Keep on like this, Hec, and you'll become a national hero!'

A national hero? Did I actually say that? It was time to go easy on the tonic.

Hector froze. 'Is it just me, or does it smell of garbage up here?'

'Uh —'

'Oh! Before I forget, Douggy, have I told you about my marvellous border wall idea?'

'Yes, and I read about it in *The Meowington Times*! Where are you going to put it, Hec?'

The Defence Secretary poured another bowlful. 'Never mind the specifics right now, I'm thinking a tiny, teeny-weeny proportion of the 4.5 billion can go towards the wall.'

Douglas felt rather merry. He also felt Hector's wet tongue grooming his neck.

'I'm so pleased we're fronting this together, Douggy. You're a brilliant minister, soon to be my Chancellor.'

'Uh, likewise.'

'We're cut from the same cloth,' purred Hector. 'You and me.'

'Indeed.'

'And none of the Westminster lot understand me like you do. By the way, I'm curious about something… where do you always disappear to in the early hours?'

Could the doolally Defence Secretary be trusted? He was a liability, but his heart was in the right place. All that stuff about blowing up the PM and finishing off General Bulgakov was the tonic talking.

'Well, I haven't ever told anyone this…'

'Mum's the word, old chap, mum's the word,' reassured Hector.

Douglas looked into his eyes. He wouldn't hurt a fly.

'A few years back, my darling little girl ran into trouble in the river. We were by the bridges and I had just given her a swimming lesson. She was doing so well, and I was so proud of her. We then had a playfight along the banks before we fell asleep…'

It felt good to finally be telling someone.

'The next thing… the next thing I remember is being

woken up by this desperate scream. And I see her flapping and struggling...'

Douglas shuddered. 'She was struggling for her life out there in the water. I'm not sure how she got out so far, she must have chased something to practice her hunting.'

His lips began quivering.

'Anyway, the current must have pulled her out. I went in as fast as I could, I dragged her out by the scruff of her neck, but it was too late. I tried and tried to resuscitate her. But it was too late, Hec. She had left me.'

Hector gave his buddy another lick. 'I am terribly sorry, dear chap.'

Douglas looked up at the sky. 'My darling Rara, I am so sorry I couldn't get to you in time. And so, I swim along that stretch by the South West London bridges every night without fail, and I will get better. I-I will make a mile soon. I will make it up to you, I have made you this promise. My darling Rara. My beautiful Rara.'

'Here's to your darling Rara,' said Hector, holding up his bowl. 'I am sure she's watching her pappah from above.'

'Thanks, Hec.' It felt good to let it all out.

'What about the mother? Is she alright?'

'Wouldn't know. She left me straight away. Tamara. She just took our things and disappeared. Stopped answering my calls, wouldn't tell me where she was, wouldn't even give me a chance to explain.'

'Brutal,' said Hector.

'One minute happily married, next minute it's all over. She accused me of murdering her child, Hec. The courts gave her everything we had.'

'Even your mansion?'

'Uh, no. Not the, uh, mansion. Anyway, the funny thing is, despite all that, I still love her.'

He felt relaxed. His friend topped up his bowl.

'I was destroyed, Hec. No legal aid from the state, couldn't even get counselling thanks to the Collective lot decimating the budgets. I now owe a fortune to some useless city lawyer. We need to change things, and Marjorie's stupid cuts are not the answer.'

Four hours had passed, they were both slumped together on their branch, out of sight from the rest of the world. The moonshot had nearly run out. 'Say, Douggy, heartfelt congratulations on your spectacular achievement!'

'Uh, which one?'

'Britain's sexiest MP. I read about it in the *Daily Mog* today.'

'Uh, pardon?'

'And I would have to agree, you look gorgeous, sir!'

'Uh, thanks! I actually had no idea.'

Five hours had passed. The moonshot was gone. 'Shlash the bureaucracy, shlash it! I love it! Ditch the bastards! Make Britain great again! By the way, did you catch my speech the other day on cherishing our glorious national gardens?'

'Ah yesh, it wash wonderful, Hec. Inshpired. It gave me butterfliesh. Thank you for writing it.' Douglas realised he was slurring his words.

The two of them, but mostly Hector, sang, and purred, and yowled into the early hours. The meeting came to an abrupt end when the Defence Secretary fell out of the treetop, and grazed his hindlegs.

✳

Douglas googled his name and there it was.

DAILY MOG
Common sense for the common cat

BRITAIN'S SEXIEST MP: SNUGGY DOUGGY CROWNED HOTTEST TOM

Backbench MP Douglas Schnitty has been voted as Britain's sexiest MP after more than a third of she-cats said he had a hot bod and admitted to fantasising about having sex with him.

Meanwhile, Shadow Health Secretary, Ophelia Peaches topped the list of she-cats, thanks to a quarter of toms finding her pouty lips sexy. Our Moggy PM came a close second with respondents saying she had nice legs, and her fashion wear was a big turn-on.

The least sexy MPs were said to be the Leader of the Opposition, Kranken, although he has a loyal fan club who adore his wacky hairdos. He polled ahead of the Minister for Welfare and Sums, Jitters Renshaw. Defence Secretary, Hector Perp Pahpousson dropped out of the top ten to twelfth place on his bed-ability ratings.

The poll was conducted by dating site, CatKiss.

Douglas stretched his midriff. Tensed his legs. All that swimming was paying off.

His head was spinning. He supped some more water.

DINNER WITH MA

Jitters' tail was trembling with excitement as he dished up his fish. It was Tuesday night, the night he got to dine with his ma, and just three days to go until his romantic getaway. Things had been going very well with Ffion on CatKiss. They had been messaging all day and night. She even seemed really interested in his debt reduction ideas. Perhaps she was the one. He couldn't wait to lick her cute little neck again.

The Minister for Welfare and General Sums was serving up a pan-fried turbot with calamari, mangoes and crushed potatoes. He loved nothing more than a buttery piece of fish with crispy skin. Jitters dined with his ma every Tuesday without fail, and he'd been looking forward to it all day.

'I think you're doing a great job, Jitsy,' said Maples. 'The bottom line is we all have to make sacrifices, don't we? No matter how tough we had it back in the day, I always made sure you never went without.'

'I'll never f-f-forget, ma.'

Maples licked her lips at the smell of the turbot. The petite British Blue had finished a gruelling two-hour shift at the hospital. 'Are you managing your workload, Jitsy? I've hardly seen you these past few weeks.'

'It's t-t-tough, ma. This s-s-sleep rule, you know, scrapping the right to 18 hours m-m-minimum s-s-sleep is deeply unpopular. Everybody hates it, on all s-s-sides.'

'Hold your nerve, Jitsy, it will be tough for a while. I mean, I sure need my 18 hours of sleep with my job, but we need to see the bigger picture.'

'I-I-It could cost us the e-e-election, ma. I might be out of a j-j-job.'

'You'll be fine, Jitsy.'

'The other d-d-day, the homeless l-l-lot living in the bins outside the office threw a carton of m-m-milk over me and called me a t-t-tosser.'

'I'm sorry, Jitsy. You know, you have the silent majority on side. I mean, I like the new Prime Minister. I love the fact that a strong she-cat has risen to the top of the country.'

'A-A-And that too a m-m-moggy. That's huge for our c-c-country.'

'And frankly, I like her story, being one of six kids, brought up on a poky tree, in an overcrowded estate, and all that.'

'Yes, we need t-t-to be making more of her b-b-backstory.'

'I think that's right. Her overall message is powerful, the shtick about remembering who we are, acting like cats again, and so on. I'd go as far as to say that she speaks to cats like me.' Maples started to purr.

'It's a b-b-breath of fresh air after the last g-g-government.'

'Definitely, Jitsy. And I love how elegant she is. OK, she may try a bit too hard with her delivery, but who cares? She gets my vote. But shh, wouldn't dare admit it to my colleagues at the hospital.'

'They'd sink their c-c-claws into you, ma.' They chuckled.

He snuggled up to her as they licked away the remnants of their supper. The crushed potatoes added a beautiful texture to the meal, he thought. Very different from the parsnip puree they had last time, both equally delicious.

Maples poured a little moonshot into her bowl.

'You know, Jitsy, we're lucky in a sense. I think back to our life when you were a kitten, and everything we went through. The useless Collective Party had made things so much worse.'

'Well, th-th-that's the principal reason why I went into p-p-politics.'

'I know, Jitsy. I will never forgive myself for letting him mistreat you in the way he did.'

'He m-m-mistreated you too, ma.'

'I felt so helpless at the situation back then. We had no help available, social services didn't have anyone to visit; the police didn't care even when I showed them the cuts and scratches all over my body. We were taxed to the hilt but somehow there was no basic help available when we really needed it.'

'It was h-h-hard.'

Maples howled softly. 'Your father loved his moonshot more than his family, and in the end, it was his precious moonshot that took him away.'

'That s-s-saved us. I would n-n-never let anything happen to you again, m-m-ma.'

Maples gave her son a gentle lick behind his ears. 'Jitsy, on a brighter note, when will you play your violin for me again?'

'I told you, ma, it's gone,' snapped Jitters. 'I h-h-haven't touched it in years.'

'That's so sad, you played so beautifully, you have so much talent. You should take it back up.'

'I'm very b-b-busy these days, what with the Prime Minister's Emergency M-M-Money Saving Committee, and my ministerial c-c-commitments.'

'I know, I know, and I'm so proud of how far you've come.'

'Thanks, ma. I owe it all t-t-to you.' He started to groom her face. 'I should also let you know that I will be unavailable this weekend. I am taking my g-g-girlfriend, Ffion, away.'

'Wow, Jitsy, girlfriend? How long have you been seeing her?'

'L-L-Long enough.'

'OK, well, that's good news, I am really pleased for you. Take it nice and slow, though, there's no rush, is there?'

'It's no b-b-big deal, but you should know. I will need to begin p-p-packing in a minute.'

'Before you go, I wanted to show you something, Jitsy. I found it the other day.' She passed her son a brown envelope with a faint stamp from his old school, St Cuthbert's. Jitters pulled out a written note.

May 2009

Dear Maples,

   I wanted to reach out to warmly congratulate you on Jitters' performance at the school assembly last week. The violin is an extremely difficult instrument to master and his rendition of the 'The Dark Forest' was incredible. He had the entire hall mesmerised. This is a complex piece, and for a kitten to put on such an emotive and dramatic performance is a real achievement. I am sure you are really proud of him. We recognise the challenges your son has with his speech and social interactions, but I hope you will take heart from this.

Jitters has the potential to go far in his violin playing, he has a real talent. He may be able to channel this into gaining more confidence. Perhaps we can meet to discuss further?

All my best,

Mrs Harrison.

'You were such a handsome cat. You were *my* handsome guy, the only British Blue in the class, and you had the most beautiful grey coat.'

Jitters' nose started quivering. He carefully folded up the letter.

'I know you had a tough time fitting in back then, but look at you now. A government minister, a potential girlfriend...'

'Thank you, ma, you always m-m-made it all better for me.'

'You worked so hard practising on that violin, day and night. I loved watching you play, watching you get lost in it, you found your inner sanctuary in it. You deserved that praise from Mrs Harrison.'

'She was my f-f-favourite.'

'Yes, she was one of the good ones. I was so happy when I received that letter, Jitsy, I remember making your favourite dinner that night.'

'K-K-Kippers with poached eggs!'

'Yes, you used to love that as a kitten.'

Maples suddenly stood up and hunched her back. Her breathing sounded heavy. She tried to gag.

She must have eaten too fast, thought Jitters.

'My, it's getting late. Time for bed, Jitsy,' she said, slinking off.

*

Almost a week since that radio interview and still not a word from the Prime Minister.

Dear Prime Minister,

Have none of your special advisers told you that it is unwise to ignore your backbenchers? We were instrumental in putting you where you are now, and we can bring about your downfall quicker you can finish one of your clumsy, er, well… clumsy sentences. What happened to our meeting to discuss those forgotten national priorities? Are you too busy snoozing in that grand residence of yours?

The Rt Hon Douglas Schnitty

He jabbed at the delete button before it accidentally sent.

Dear Prime Minister,

Following on from my last email, are you available tomorrow evening for our meeting to discuss funding for the forgotten national priorities you spoke of? Some of them need urgent attention as you are aware. Very happy to make written recommendations for your consideration and help in any way I can.

Warmest wishes,

The Rt Hon Douglas Schnitty

DILEMMA IN
THE CHAPEL

THUD! The book of prayer fell on the floor, rudely awakening Douglas from his snooze. It was the best sleep he'd had in days. He felt so snug in the chapel. The warm chapel. At peace. Ruined by some idiot.

'Oh, hello, D-D-Douglas, or sh-sh-sh-should I say Britain's s-s-sexiest MP?'

It was that Jitters, what the hell did he want?

The grey British Blue leapt up next to him, with too much energy.

'I-I-Is everything OK? Y-Y-You look a bit rough. W-W-Worse for wear.'

'I'm fine, Jitters, I'd just nodded off.'

'Ooh, is that your s-s-supper?'

'No! That's my good friend, Shuffles.'

'A fish?'

'Yes, a fish.'

'Are they allowed in ch-ch-chapels?'

'What can I do for you, Jitters?'

Douglas stretched his achy leg out.

'Glad I b-b-bumped into you.' Jitters proceeded to drone

on about his important role in the Emergency Money Saving Committee, his optimism on Marjorie's election prospects, his views on her character, she was a kind soul, he said. She had the country's interests at heart apparently. Douglas' eyes felt heavy. He caught something about a leadership challenge and crazy old Hector. He jolted upright.

'I-I-Is it true th-th-that he planned to assassinate her?' he asked.

'Uh, no, Jitters, where did you hear that?'

'I have my s-s-sources. Heard you had to t-t-talk him out of it.'

'No, Jitters, he was as drunk as a skunk that night and he got a bit carried away. It was the moonshot talking.'

'It's j-j-just…'

'Just what?'

'Well, he is making a p-p-play for the top job.'

'Oh yeah?'

'He treated me t-t-to a fish dinner. It was, well, rather f-f-fancy. He kept mentioning the "n" word.'

'The "n" word?'

'Yes, n-n-nukes.'

'Hmm. Glad to hear he was being his authentic moon-shotty self.'

'He also wants to give me a t-t-top ministerial role.'

'Does he now?'

'Yes.'

'Will you accept?'

'There's n-n-no vacancy.'

'There may be soon, Jitters.'

'Everyone wants to be in his C-C-Cabinet.'

'Yep, he's certainly the hot ticket right now. Might not be such a bad thing.'

'But I b-b-believe in Marjorie, sh-sh-she's trying to do the right thing. Sh-Sh-She is courageous. Not trying to chase p-p-popularity polls.'

'She needs to help the needy. There are so many cats living in the bins, they're dying, Jitters. It will become her legacy. What if Hector can save them? Channel his madness into good?'

'We will only be able to help the n-n-needy once our f-f-finances are under c-c-control. It's s-s-simple economics.'

Same old Jitters, thought Douglas. *Blindly loyal to his master. Parroting the same old tired and predictable lines. A career politician if ever there was one.*

'Is it just m-m-me or does something smell a bit rotten?'

'Uh...'

'Like a d-d-dead rat.'

The Minister for Welfare and General Sums rolled over and started purring. 'H-H-Hector said I can have a-a-any job I want in his C-C-Cabinet. Said I was a rising s-s-star.'

Douglas made up some unnecessarily elaborate excuse about being late for an appointment with the dental hygienist, who was supposedly at her wits end with him, and got out of there. He would go to the river a little earlier tonight and pop by his and Rara's special spot. He was sure she would be there.

His head was spinning. Still nothing from the PM since his interview a week ago. Not even an acknowledgement of his emails. Perhaps it was now time to put his faith in Hector, jump on the bandwagon, after all it seemed unstoppable.

Surely, he was all bluster with the whole nuke thing. Maybe he could be the one to sort out the country with his no bullshit approach, be a real friend to the homeless. A breath of fresh air. He could be kept in line with a strong team around him. He could become a hero with the right guidance. Surely anyone was better than the hopeless Marjorie? He'd talk it through with his darling Rara, she always helped him do the right thing.

*

THE MEOWINGTON TIMES

OPINION: MAKE BRITAIN GREAT AGAIN – BY HECTOR PERP PAHPOUSSON, DEFENCE SECRETARY.

My dear friends, we have won the lottery of life! We are the smartest species ever to inhabit land; we possess the most superior of minds. Think about it, we can do everything the ancient hoomans could do, and a whole lot more. Yes, we can read and write; we can recite beautiful poetry, and we can dance like angels. We can fly planes and launch missiles; and we are better drivers than they ever were. While they stumbled clumsily through their sorry day-to-day existence with their dangly arms and wobbly heads, we observed quietly and we took notes. We played cutesies with them, we feigned helplessness, while ensuring we were always topped up and waited on.

Friends, over the decades, we've evolved to laugh, and cry, make all sorts of wonderful expressions with our faces, and show all manner of emotions. But when needs must, we can hunt, climb, and attack with ferocity. There is nothing that can stop us as a species from thriving.

So, I am most bemused to see that despite all this, we Brits have allowed ourselves to be held back and strangled by the regulations and bureaucracy of the elitist Global Cats Alliance. But despair not, my fellow country toms and shes, we have a once in a lifetime opportunity to break free from the chokehold. If you are as excited as I am by this prospect, write to your MP, with the words: 'LISTEN TO HECTOR AND SAY GOODBYE TO THE GLOBAL CATS ALLIANCE.' Do it today. Then we can get on, build ourselves a better future (and a wall), and make Britain Great again!

Douglas rolled up the paper and checked his emails. There were more than 150 messages already in his inbox advising him to listen to Hector. He certainly knew how to stir the masses.

HECTOR'S MOMENT

It felt lively in the lair of the Black Cats. There was Hector, reclining in his usual spot at the front, bathing in the attention. The herd fought amongst itself shoving various moonshot offerings under his nose. Word had got round of a sizeable donor backing the Defence Secretary to become the next leader, none other than the owner of the well renowned Pawchester Hotel Group. The coffers were filling up nicely, and his Cabinet was oversubscribed.

There was Mukerjee, dressed all in black, skulking in the background. The Society Elder concealed himself in the shadows and watched on at the fracas. You had to be incredibly brave or very stupid to allow yourself to outshine him.

Douglas eavesdropped on the hushed chatter next to him. There was talk from the new Black Ops Unit that the leader of the opposition, Kranken, was associating himself with some rather unsavoury characters who wanted to introduce communism into the country. The Unit had decided to dig up the dirt on the old tom, and drip feed it to *The Meowington Times* between now and the election.

Douglas forced his way through the adoring mob. 'It's the tomcat of the moment!'

'Ah, there you are, sir!' Hector jolted upright and saluted with his left paw. 'Shit! I mean sit! Try this one. It's rare and most creamy. Can you feel the hint of… liquorish?'

Douglas topped up the podgy black chinchilla's bowl. It must easily have been his tenth. 'Are you slurring your words there, Hec? Just kidding. This stuff never fails to, uh, bring out the authentic you.'

The minister in charge of defence rose and stretched his legs. His expression turned serious. 'Matured in French oak, you know. Pour another for yourself, old chap. I wouldn't share this stuff with anyone else. Not even Lord Mukerjee over there.'

He plonked next to Douglas, leaning into his pal. 'So, tonight's the night. I'm excited, Douggy.' He began rolling some nip leaf. 'I'm excited for us. The dream union.'

'Me too, Hec. Remember not to hold back. Mention the wall too, it will play well with this crowd. And it will keep the cheques coming.'

Hector stroked his whiskers. 'I've actually been doing the sums on the first phase of construction for the wall, and the good news is that —'

'Quiet!' shouted Mukerjee, standing at the podium.

Huh-hum-huh-huh
Huh-hum-huh-huh.

We sit strong and proud
We see things nobody sees.

The sea of black cats began chanting.

We feast like kings
We make our Mews

We fend for ourselves.

We're everywhere you look
And we're nowhere to be found.

Om-yah-mew-mew
Biladi, Katze, Mao.

As per tradition, the chanting went on for several minutes and grew louder and louder before the familiar clash of the giant cymbals brought the lair to silence.

'Next item on the agenda is an updaaaate from the Defence Secretary on the Global Cats Alliaaaaance project.'

Hector rose confidently and stretched his body. He swaggered to the front.

'Ultimately,' he began. 'Ultimately, we need to convince our glorious leader to walk from the Global Cats Alliance. Our membership in it is a folly. Spending 4.5 billion British Mews in our lifetime is bonkers when that money could go on our defences and make us strong again.'

Douglas gave him a reassuring nod.

'Now Marjorie, our dear Prime Minister, and her clique of yes men will tell you that we need a vote on this, we need a dedicated unit set up, it's a big decision, blah blah blah.'

Hector stumbled. 'Oops. My dear friends, we don't need any delay. The Global Alliance is an unnecessary and costly endeavour. Leaving it needs to become a flagship policy in our upcoming election manifesto, and then we begin our exit operation as soon as we're re-elected. Hopefully with a stonking majority, if she can manage it.'

He seemed buoyed by the nods of approval from across the lair.

'And once we are out, we can build a wall! A beautiful, shiny, marvellous wall to... to... I digress. Before any of that, we need to make the Prime Minister see sense.'

He lowered his voice. 'Time to launch our campaign, get the public excited. Once they get behind us, she'll have no choice but to yield. We'll bare our teeth at the bastards, and together we will change our country for the better.'

Cheers erupted in the lair.

'And so, my dear friend Douglas and I have worked on a slogan for the project.' Hector tripped and took a tumble as he approached the red velvet curtains for the grand reveal. 'Behold!' He lunged and pulled them back with his teeth.

Toodle-oo, Global Cats Alliance. We're off to build a better future (and a beautiful wall).

'Well, what do we think?'

There was a silence. It was now or never. 'Uh, fucking idiotic,' Douglas said with as much conviction as he could muster.

Hector froze.

It had to be done. Yes, we were facing a homeless crisis, he'd seen the latest figures this morning, another 11,000 officially living in the bins. Something drastic was needed. But putting a nutter in charge wasn't the answer. It had become blindly obvious that he didn't give two hoots about the needy. Marjorie was bad, but this guy would be a complete disaster.

'Uh, it doesn't make sense,' continued Douglas. 'And this lunatic Defence Secretary is most certainly not the right cat for this important project. He doesn't have the right temperament to get this done. He's bananas!'

Hector glared over. He looked aghast. 'Douggy?'

'Sorry, Hec, nothing personal. But this is too important for our country.'

The lair fell silent. 'And we need a proper leader for it. Someone who doesn't slur his words and bang on about cuckoo ideas such as building a wall. Which, by the way, isn't even your brief.'

Hector's hairs stood on edge. 'What the hell are you doing, old chap?'

'Just doing what needs to be done. You can't just string crazy sentences together to get noticed. Now if I was tasked with leading this project, I would get straight to the point on the serious stuff. Such as how we plan to use the billions that we save to improve lives.'

The cat in charge of the nation's defence was trembling like a jelly. He crept over, eyeballing Douglas, claws out.

'You traitor,' he hissed. 'You are… you are betraying me, stabbing me very deliberately in the front. Twisting the knife.'

Dozens of wide-eyed black cats were fixated on Douglas. Following his every word, his every move.

'Oh, enough of the dramatics,' replied Douglas, almost melodically. This was not as bad as he had feared. 'I wanted you to succeed, really I did. But you are mad. Jingoistic. You will get us nuked —'

'Traitor!' growled Hector, his tail puffed up. The two cats circled slowly around each other.

'And by the way, Hec, there is no such thing as a *beautiful wall*. The whole idea is barmy. And we live on a bloody island in case you hadn't noticed.'

'What?' said Hector.

'Silence!' Mukerjee stepped in between the feuding duo.

'You're a ghastly fellow, Douglas Schnitty,' screamed Hector.

It was time to deliver the knockout blow. 'Well, Hec, you're a hypocrite. You blather on about immigrants, but you do realise that you come from a family of immigrants yourself?'

'What?'

'You heard!'

'Pish posh! I am a Chinchilla through and through, we originate from a fine —'

'Uh, you're a Chinchilla *mix*, and a conveniently deaf one too,' Douglas continued, fixing his stare onto the Defence Secretary. 'I've looked into your ancestry; it involved a tomcat mixing with a Persian.'

'That's absurd!' screamed Hector.

'Explains why you're pure black. Purebred Chinchillas cannot be your colour! Now, there's nothing wrong with that, it's just that you're a hypocrite!'

'I am special, the only pure black Chinchilla to exist. Anywhere in the world, I'll have you know!'

'You're deluded, Hector Pahpousson —'

'And I do find it difficult to hear. I have an ear condition from an injury back when I was leading a rescue mission in the army.'

'You're deluded. You rant on about immigration, but you're a descendant from immigrants yourself. Oh, the irony —'

'Speaking of colourings, you are hardly pure black...' Hector looked around, 'Friends, the rules state that one must have at least 90 per cent of pure black colouring to be eligible to join the Black Cats Society. This common tom is a fraud, the ginge all over his neck and chest makes up for at least 15 per cent —'

Douglas had never seen so many wide-awake cats in one place before. Anywhere. Ever. There must have been about 200 big, wide, shocked eyes surrounding him; not a single snoozer.

'Sil-eeence!' shouted Mukerjee. 'Well, this is rather an unexpected development, isn't it? We don't want to rush a decision on such an important project such as leaving the Global Alliance, and we don't *need* to rush it.'

Hector's long-haired, black, bushy tail was puffed up and quivering.

'We must get the leader right,' continued Mukerjee, 'then the plan, then the slogan. One thing at a time, in an orderly manner. The good news is that we have time on our side, time to think this all through.'

He circled around the pair and nudged each affectionately with his head. 'Stick together, the two of you. We Black Cats are strongest when united. My decision is that we will postpone this business until after the election. The PM has already committed to giving it a serious look, and heaven help her if she were to go back on her word. Let's see how things play out.'

HELPER WANTED!

Hector was sitting in his office wailing loudly. He'd been wailing for three days since the betrayal of the century. He was wounded, shocked. The country would soon learn of the gross injustice he had suffered, the masses would revolt. He had liked Douglas, he'd trusted him. He had given that wretched tom his moonshot, and that too the pricey stuff. *Traitor!* He thrashed his tail onto his desk viciously. *Thud!*

It was time to snap out of it. He took a breath and grabbed his bamboo comb. He ran his paw over the engraved lettering: *semper invicta*. Always undefeated. He began combing his luscious whiskers methodically. Douglas would rue the moment he got up in front of the Society and stabbed him so ruthlessly. Stabbed him and twisted the knife. He would now work night and day to deliver revenge, sweet revenge.

The Shanghai Symphony was on full blast. The sound of the orchestra was spectacular, almost threatening, just like his mood. Yes, it was time to cook up a storm, turn things up a notch, and he wasn't talking about the orchestra. He stomped over to his gold-plated cream fountain and lay under it, letting the cream splatter onto him from head to toe. The dollops were therapeutic.

He picked up his pocket mirror, his piercing blue eyes staring straight back at him beneath his soggy long hair caked in cream. It was time to respond. The orchestra was such a tour de force, the very opposite of his new enemy, the slimeball at the top of his hit list. Back in the army he would have been well and truly humiliated, he would have had his ear bitten off for treachery.

It was time to make an important call. He licked the cream off his phone and looked up his old mate from the Royal Tank Regiment. 'Greetings, Hoole, Hec speaking. Well, how the bloody hell are you, old chap?'

Whatever had happened back in those days, he could always rely on his old buddy Hoole. He was a good guy, he always delivered. Those were the days, the peak of his youth, shock action his speciality, she-cats fighting over him, life was so carefree.

'I need a favour, sir! I need to get my paws on a tank!' His old friend was umming and ahhing. 'I need to demonstrate a bit of shock action to overwhelm an enemy, just like the old days. I've been wronged.' He licked his lips.

He could have made General by now. Oh, if only it hadn't ended that way. Hector hoisted himself up. *Enough of that, the whole sorry episode was a long time ago. Time now to focus on sweet and sophisticated revenge. The wounded hero will rise and prevail. Always undefeated.* He curled up and began bawling again. Bawling through the night, just like the night before, and the night before that.

*

Meanwhile Douglas had finally been invited back to Downing Street. He peeked over at the Prime Minister as he lay opposite her. It was all very well for her to be sprawled out in her grand study, garbed in her fancy shawl.

'Say, Prime Minister, did you hear about the shenanigans at the Society meeting the other night?'

'Yes, word has reached me that you handled it, Douglas, and I wanted to thank you.'

Finally, a thank you for something. She owed him alright.

'No problem, Prime Minister. Like I said, don't worry about that Hector. He's all bluster.'

She looked distracted. He took his moment.

'Uh, Prime Minister, about that potential 50 million for our forgotten national priorities, shall we begin with —'

Marjorie rolled over onto her side. 'You know, Douglas, I've been thinking. You're smart, you're reliable, the more I get to know you, the more I, er... well, like you.'

'Uh, likewise, Prime Minister.' There was something sad about her, a bit lonely. He felt sorry for her. 'Uh, I'm your friend!' he spluttered, without thinking.

'Pardon?'

'Uh, sorry, Prime Minister, just wanted to say that I'm your friend, that's all.'

'Thank you, Douglas, and I see you as a friend too.'

'So, about these, uh, priorities —'

'Douglas, it's been a very tough day. I'm sorry but could we have this discussion another time?'

Another time? Why did you invite me over then, he felt like screaming in her face.

'I should be able to make some time in the diary in the

next couple of days,' she said. 'You can update me on your constituent, er… Mandy then too.'

'That's fine,' he muttered, getting up abruptly.

'Do you have somewhere to be?'

'Uh —'

'Stay and have a drink with me, Douglas.'

He sat back down. It was frustrating but she wasn't all bad. She'd remembered Mandy's name which was a pleasant surprise. He tried to think of something nice to say to her.

'Your, uh, décor is first class.'

Décor? First class? Why did I say that? What the hell is wrong with me?

'Thank you, Douglas. That's the nicest thing anyone has said to me all week.'

'I, uh, love what you've done here in your study,' he continued. 'All the red and gold you have going on, it's regal. Matches your dress sense too. You're definitely the most, uh, fashionable Prime Minister we've ever had. Honestly, how have you not got suitors lining up for you?'

Marjorie turned her back on him.

Shucks, too far.

'Uh, I'm sorry, Prime Minister, I didn't mean to cross a line.' He got back up, 'I should probably get going.'

'No, wait, Douglas. It is fine.' She poured moonshot into two crystal bowls. 'I have not told anyone what I am about to tell you. I, er… well, I came out of a long-term relationship not very long ago.'

Blimey, thought Douglas.

'It was hell,' she continued. 'Every day, there was a fight about something. I knew from the beginning we were very different, our entire outlook on life was so very different. You know, our backgrounds were different.'

'Uh, that sucks, I'm sorry, Prime Minister. But look on the bright side —'

'I'll never forget how once he just deserted me in the middle of a dance. And all over some stupid, nonsensical fight over biting one's kids. I mean is it so bad to say you would give your kitty a little nip on their hind legs if they were to play up?'

'Hardly child abuse,' muttered Douglas.

'Yes, indeed. I got one or two nips in my time, and it did me no harm!'

Well, that's debateable, thought Douglas, fighting back a grin.

'Anyway, he shouted at me and declared that he could never marry someone who would treat his kittens like that. And then he stormed off and went home. I was devastated.'

'Well, that's no way to treat a catess. He clearly had no idea how lucky he was.'

'I was humiliated, Douglas. I fell for him as soon as I had laid my eyes on him. He could be such a charmer and he had that cute moody thing going on. But then I noticed he would, er… he would grimace whenever I spoke.'

'Sounds like you're clearly better off without him.'

'Yes, and he was a real lefty.'

Douglas scoffed.

'He used to announce his opinions in public all the time. It got embarrassing. We even moved in together, into a houseboat. Looking back, we were too rash with the boat thing. I just… well, I felt so happy when I was in it. It was our home, you know?'

'Well, look at you now. You're the Prime Minister! Residing at the world's most famous address!'

'Yes. You know, I never in my wildest dreams would have thought, even five years ago, that one day I would, er... well, that I would be living in a boat on the Thames, let alone at Number Ten Downing Street! Such a far cry from the rough tree estate I grew up in with my mother.'

'So, what happened in the end, Prime Minister?'

'Well, I was in love with him, but it would never have worked. Anyway, it's getting late, and I wanted to ask you something, Douglas.' Marjorie sidled up next to him.

Oh god, what's happening? He flinched involuntarily.

'Like I say, you're smart, you're reliable, and I wonder whether you would like to be my number two?'

'Uh, number two? As in...'

'As in my deputy, Douglas. You would officially be on my team and working closely with me. As the Deputy Prime Minister.'

Careful, he warned himself. *Don't want to get tainted by her harsh cuts agenda, become a sell-out.*

'Uh...'

Doing the right thing, saving the homeless was more important than a fancy title. Even if it did come with a ministerial office. A cosy, warm, ministerial office. A roof over his head.

'Uh...'

He stroked his whiskers.

'Uh...'

Must do the right thing. He owed it to the thousands suffering, like Mandy.

'Well, Douglas?'

At least she had remembered Mandy's name, that was something.

'Douglas? Hello? You'll of course get your old office back. Effective immediately.'

'I'd be delighted to accept, Prime Minister. I am honoured to be asked to serve you as your Deputy. Humbled.'

He was late for his nightly river swim, but first he had to get his advert sorted.

Wanted! A helper to assist with day to day thinking and certain administrative tasks. Someone bright and enthusiastic to plan and deliver special projects. You will be expected to undertake activities of a top-secret nature. Discretion is a must, chutzpah very much desired. Above all, a hunger to win is essential. Apply with a short covering letter, accompanied with a remittance of a dozen cream eclairs. Interviews will take place in my den. You will be richly compensated.

MOVING OUT DAY

'Gah, politician guy, yaaah!' cried the elderly she-cat neighbour, jerking her head wildly.

'Uh, yes. Sorry to bother you, miss,' said Douglas.

She was scratching away. 'Haaah, whaaa-dyaaa want?'

Douglas crushed two pills onto some chicken. 'Here, take this. You need to keep up your food intake. And these meds are extra strong, they'll get rid of your parasites within hours. Take another two tomorrow.'

'Waaah, thaaaa-thaaaank you.'

'It's no problem at all.'

She seemed to be signalling something. 'Gaaaah, gaaaaangs hah-hah-have —'

'The gangs?'

'Yaaaah! Hah-have —' She flicked her tail towards his patch.

'They've been back?'

'Yaaah!'

She looked worried and gabbled away hysterically.

'Shh, don't worry,' he whispered, 'I'm leaving today. But look after yourself, OK? I will come back and check on you soon.'

He threw his shirts, his case files, and his few worldly

possessions onto an abandoned trolley. He could hear Shuffles doing her thing. 'You'll be back in your palace really soon, little one.'

He heard a scratch on the bin. 'Mr Schnitty? Sir?'

'Come in, kittie.'

The ginger kitten dumped a satchel stuffed with envelopes.

'Good work, kittie. Did you deliver all the parcels?'

'Yessir.'

'And did Maples get her package.'

'Yessir. She told me to thank you for your kindness. She said she's doing better today.'

'Good.'

'And look, sir!' He dropped a mouse at Douglas' paws.

'Wow! Did you catch this?'

'Yessir! Me and my mate have been practising what you teached us!'

'Taught us. It's taught, not teached.'

'What you taught us. I caught a pigeon too.'

'I'm proud of you. Make sure you share it with your family, though. And offer some to your neighbours from time to time. And do me a favour please, catch some for the she-cat next door. She doesn't know how to hunt and she's poorly.'

The young cat started bouncing around. 'Yessir, I will.'

'Good, don't forget.'

'I won't, I promise.'

There we go, thought Douglas, a perfect example of communities looking out for each other. That's what we needed to talk about on the doorstep. We could call it the Big Society. The public would get it.

'I must go now, sir, mummy says I have homework to do.'

'One moment, I have something for you. Hold out your paw.' Douglas took off his watch.

'Is this for me?'

'Yes. Look after it.'

'Oh wow! Thank you, sir!' He gave Douglas a peck on his forehead and scrambled off.

Douglas took in a deep breath. He was feeling inexplicably low. He would miss this place in a funny way. He would miss the nice kittens he'd met and the stars at night. He'd even got used to the stink of rotten eggs. He looked over at his crazy neighbour. She was staring right back at him, wide-eyed. She scrambled over and nudged him affectionately, almost knocking him over. He'd be back to give her some good news hopefully very soon. He had written to the council last week, demanding tree housing for her. She was an urgent case, and they had promised to fast track her. He looked around one final time and started to yank the string tied onto the trolley.

UNIVERSAL BASIC INCOME

'What's this, then?'

'Grilled mouse bites.'

'And this?'

'Pigeon Bakewell.'

'I'll take the Bakewell with my usual latte. Milky.'

'Of course.'

Well, that's awkward, observed Jitters. That Kranken was back again and getting a rather frosty reception from Pierre. What a state he was, all dishevelled and gap-toothed.

Jitters put on his aviators. He wouldn't be recognised in them. He went back to his balance sheet. He had got as far as writing *National Income vs Expenditure.* He glanced at his phone, nothing. His new love interest, Ffion, seemed to be playing it cool.

Pierre walked past and set the coffee and cake on the table across from him. Kranken scowled at the Bakewell. 'OK, ready? Welcome to the Krankcast.'

Pierre inched closer, hesitantly. Jitters minimised the spreadsheet on his laptop.

'Now then, you know how we all want a just and equal society? And my guest will recall our conversation from last time —'

'Oh no, not this again,' Pierre uttered.

'Hear me out, please. I can reveal exclusively to you, dear listener, that we will bring in a 2,000-British-Mew income for everybody.'

'Non. Stop this recording.'

'Oh, for goodness' sake, why? I'm talking about a monthly, unconditional payment. Regardless of your earnings or employment status.'

'L'universal basic income?' Pierre rolled his eyes.

'Yeah. It will be a flagship policy in my manifesto. You see, my mission is to end poverty in this country. And lemme tell you, if we give everyone money, they're no longer poor. I swear it will work.'

'No, not simple. I don't like this. It would create many problems for businesses like mine.'

'But why?' snapped Kranken. 'It would give employees everywhere security, and they'd have real power and say over things like their earnings and working conditions. Happy and more secure workers would —'

'Monsieur, I have to stop you there. And please stop shouting. I appreciate my team very much and I am proud to pay them well. We are a, what you call this thing, a happy ship.'

'Yeah, but why settle for a piddly 10-British-Mew per hour job, hypothetically speaking, Pierre, when workers could receive a basic income? It would give them the power to command much more! Power to the masses!' Kranken leapt onto the table.

'Monsieur, please keep off the tables.'

'You'd benefit from the universal income too, I swear to you. It is *universal*, right? As it says on the tin.'

'I must say it's not for me, sorry. Maybe try talking to some other businesses? There are plenty of good delis around, I can recommend a few to you —'

'I'm still talking! We really need to change the way we think as a society. Did you know they are trialling this excellent idea all round the world? The Persians, the Siamese, even the Norwegian Forest Cats are looking at it.'

'Yes, yes, but it is truly a terrible idea. Think about it, why would someone want to come and work for me if they are getting free money for doing nothing? It will kill aspiration. And how are you going to pay for it exactly?'

'Well, the need for welfare will be eliminated, and that alone will save the country billions.' Kranken beamed.

'So, you are going to get rid of welfare payments, the money meant for the poorest, and you are going to redistribute that amongst everyone, including cats like me? It sounds very hoomanist.'

'Psst!' Kranken beckoned Pierre's two members of staff over.

'What are you doing?' The irritation in Pierre's voice was beginning to show.

'I'd like to hold a quick informal focus group to test this idea.'

Pierre turned to French. 'Non, non, non. S'il te plait, ignore-le' — *please ignore him.*

'Juste sourir et hocher' — *just smile and nod.*

'Ignorer le fou' — *ignore the fool.*

'Look, so many cats will have the financial security to really think about what they wanna do with their life. Perhaps they don't wanna serve coffees, perhaps they wanna own the damn coffee shops! Just like you!'

'That's all well and good, but money is not a right, my friend. It should be earnt. I took out a big loan to get this place up and running, and I worked six-hour shifts for many years.'

'But what if you didn't have to go through all that? And don't take this the wrong way, Pierre, but you are all looking rather stressed. Perhaps if you lot enjoyed a universal income, you would all be happier, and that —'

'I think what would make me happy is if you leave. Just go. Now. Please.'

'But what about my podcast?'

'Please go.'

'I'm gonna have to start looking for another guest.'

'Take le milky coffee with you.'

'I will give you some time, you'll come round.'

'Just do me a favour please – don't come back for a while. Take a break from here, oui?'

'Oh well, at least I'll save hundreds of British Mews making my lattes at home.'

'Imbecile.'

Jitters started writing an email.

I've got something for you. It's big. The Cats Collective want to introduce a Universal Basic Income of 2,000 British Mews, per month, to every cat. It will be in their manifesto. Kranken was sounding out the local

deli owner. It didn't end well, he got kicked out! We now know two of their flagship election pledges. They are both non-starters, completely unaffordable. We have nothing to worry about.
Jitters.

His boss would be pleased with that.

BAD HAPPENS

Douglas sat next to his clownfish friend. It felt odd being back in the den, it was pokier and dingier than he'd remembered. He stretched out without thinking and the pile of fish food came tumbling down again. At least it smelt a bit better than the slums, and it was warm, and Shuffles had her space back. They had both finished their dessert, and it was time for the evening entertainment.

The Deputy Prime Minister squinted at the grainy footage of the shadow cabinet gathering. Their Westminster headquarters looked crummy. They looked anxious, and a little grumpy, as they filed into their tiny room. It looked even crummier than his own crummy little four by four, it looked like a box.

Douglas squinted at a large object in the corner of the screen. It was wrapped in brown paper and had a red bow on the front. None of them seemed to be going near it or touching it, they were whispering and glancing at it. Looked a bit suspect.

'Thanks for being here, it's late, and believe me I don't wanna be here anymore than you do,' said a gruff voice.

It was that Kranken, Mr Leader of the Opposition, slinking in with a suitcase. He'd shaved the sides of his head, leaving a ginger tuft at the top and back, like the mohawk styles the hoomans used to sport. He needed to sack his image consultant. And hairdresser.

'Right, listen, I promised you something very special last week, so let's get on with it, alright?'

There was a silence in the room. Spirits seemed low. No surprise as the election was just over a month away, and every poll had the Cats Collective trailing by double digit numbers.

'I wanna share with you something close to my heart,' continued Kranken. 'Something I've been developing over the past few days, ever since that witch called her stupid election. Something that's about to turn our fortunes around.'

He ripped off the brown paper to reveal a huge stone tablet. It looked at least ten feet tall. Douglas made out the words *BAD HAPPENS (But we'll make it better)* carved into the front.

'What the hell is that?' came a voice from the back.

'How much did it cost?' came another.

'20K all in, including delivery, and they threw in my signature at the bottom for free.' Kranken looked pleased with himself. 'Look,' he continued. 'We need to put our vision out there, be clear about the reason we exist as the Cats Collective.'

The audio was hissy. Douglas could just about hear what was being said. He made a mental note that the transmitter needed moving for the next time.

'We desperately need to look out for each other, right? Embrace each other,' Kranken prattled on. 'If we, cats, wanna truly prosper, then we've gotta grow and evolve, and frankly stop being such greedy and selfish pigs. And we shouldn't be afraid to say it.'

'Great, but what's with the stone?' yelled someone.

'Well, we need to make a statement, get noticed, have a purpose. Now we have a slogan, and it is carved into stone. Soon it will be etched into the nation's memory.'

'Yeah, but... bad... happens?' cried someone else. 'I don't... I don't geddit.'

'Well then, let me explain,' Kranken growled. 'My life has taught me one important lesson over and over again. That bad happens. And we can't stop it. With this mess of a government, lots of bad happens to lots of us. It's sickening! Our purpose, colleagues, is to make it better. That's what the country wants —'

'Wharra a load of crap!'

'I'm still speaking! Bad happens, but we, the Cats Collective, will make it better. Vote for *us* to make it better for *you*.'

'It doesn't make sense,' someone whined. 'Bad happens. It sounds illiterate.'

'What are you talking about?' hissed Kranken. 'It's simple, it's relatable, and I swear the public will instantly understand it. In fact, I'm gonna talk about this on my next podcast episode.'

'You can call it the Krankstone, geddit? Krank-stone!' Nervous laughter erupted in the room.

'Where are you going to put it?'

'Does that really matter at this point in time?' Kranken looked as if he was about to claw his entire Cabinet. 'Well, now that you ask, we are gonna keep it right here, in our HQ.

And it will stay here until every single one of us is living and breathing the message, reciting it in our sleep! And when the time comes, it will be proudly displayed in the middle of Downing Street.'

'What's in the suitcase, then?' came another question.

'Some biscuits. Chicken biscuits.'

'This is bollocks. I'm off, bye!'

'Quiet please! We need to give the country a clear reason to vote for us. And this is it. It's powerful.'

Kranken stood underneath the stone and look up at it adoringly. 'From now on, everything we do and everything we talk about, will be guided by this principle. It will be our election slogan. It needs to go through every letterbox in the country.'

'And on billboards,' shouted Ophelia. 'Through the letterboxes and on the billboards!'

'You're shouting, Ophelia,' snapped Kranken.

'Sorry, Leader. And let's not forget 50,000 life coaches for the country will make things better! It fits. Like a glove. Ears!'

'What do you mean, ears?'

'Ears! As in affirmative! As in very well!'

Kranken scowled. 'It's yes, not ears. And we still ain't got enough policies to make a manifesto. The election is just five weeks away. I've asked you all for submissions and they were bloody stupid and embarrassing. Half of them were littered with spelling and grammar mistakes. We can't even flipping well write —'

'Yes, thinking caps on please, colleagues!' interrupted Ophelia. 'We can totally beat the Freedom Cat scum in five weeks' time. If you want inspiration, just take a look at my detailed life coach policy. In case you're wondering, it just came to me one morning. A flash of genius, one could say. Ears!'

Kranken bared his teeth and edged towards her.

'The masses won't mind paying a little more in taxes to fund life coaches for the nation,' she continued. 'They will help us realise that we can all achieve our dreams, no matter where we come from.'

'Enough of the damn life coaches!' hissed Kranken. 'The public don't like it.'

The room had almost emptied. 'Ophelia too must be off now,' she declared. 'It's my little Portia's birthday and I need to get hold of some cod fillets, candles, and muscovado sugar. I'm baking her a cod loaf. It's her favourite.'

Douglas rolled over on the floor cackling uncontrollably. He pulled the wire out of the socket. The TV zapped off. Kranken and his lefty Collective Party would soon be laughed into oblivion. One day our kittens would learn all about their crackpot ideas at school, it would give them something to laugh about at playtime. Perhaps that Krank could have his very own chapter in the history books. After the one on the disastrous fate of the hoomans.

He stretched out for his burner phone and began typing:

> Angus, here's a juicy scandal for you to splash on your political pages – Cats Collective have shelled out 20K on a massive stone tablet with the words "BAD HAPPENS" etched on it. It's their election slogan. That Krank wants to move it to Downing Street if they win. Went

down badly at their meeting this evening. Entire shadow cabinet walked out in disgust. I kid you not. There is talk of booting him out before election – Anon.

*

Jitters reclined in one of the country's finest napping rooms at the romantic Cornish retreat. He had reserved the most expensive luxury feather ball for two, and he wasn't going to waste it. He looked around, he had the whole room to himself. His nose hurt from its excessive twitching, something that happened whenever he was upset. The flute music, warm milk and candlelight inside the napping rooms helped calm it.

He was tired after the long train journey. He'd spent it doing a cost-benefit analysis of extending the working day from two to three hours, and from two to four hours. The PM would be pleased with the productivity figures he had generated, the policy would fire up the economy.

He was gutted that Ffion had bailed on him at the last minute. And that too by message on CatKiss, she didn't even have the decency to call. Something about not being ready to get involved with another tom so soon after her nasty breakup. That's the first he'd heard about any breakup.

He sniffed on his special blanky. It was as if his ma was right there. It had her scent on it and it made him feel better. He was pleased he'd remembered to pack it.

He thought about the message again. She said he was a nice guy, but apparently his outlook on life was incompatible with hers. It was her words about his ma that hurt the most. She found it strange that a grown cat lived with his mother and spoke about her so much. She said it was something she couldn't get used to. Well, he wouldn't apologise about that. He felt sorry for her. She obviously wasn't fortunate enough to experience such a strong bond in her life.

He had tried calling her but no response. Eighteen times on the train down to be precise. She could at least do the right thing and speak to him, explain herself. He logged onto CatKiss again. She had seen all his messages, but nothing. *You can still join me here,* he typed. *It's not too late. Just get the train up. Please. I've already bought you a ticket. Let's give us a chance, just talk things through and enjoy ourselves. We can share a pigeon pie. What do you say?*

Maybe it was time to pack in the whole dating thing. The she-cats on the app were weird. They either returned his slow blinks, flirted a bit, and then went quiet suddenly. Or they just went quiet after a few messages. No explanation. One of them even blocked him after he told her what he did for a living. *Brutal.*

Well, whatever happened with this one, Jitters would stay the whole weekend. And he would tell his ma they had a great time together. She had been on cloud nine all week. No need to worry or upset her. Besides, things could still work out. He hit refresh on his messages again. *I am devastated Ffion. It doesn't have to be like this. I can change. Come and join me, please.*

*

Douglas spotted an email from his boss. It said: *Re: Our forgotten national priorities* in the subject header. Finally! His heart started thumping.

> *Dear Douglas,*
>
> *I'm sorry I have been so slow to come back to you on this. I suggest we park any discussion on funding other national priorities for now. Most immediately, we need to prepare for our upcoming meeting with the President of the Global Alliance. It may well turn out that we are successful in our negotiations, and we can therefore remain in the Alliance, in which case the whole issue of our membership money will become a moot point. In any case, my Emergency Money Saving Committee is insisting we need every British Mew committed to paying down our debts. Indeed, until things become clearer, this must remain our sole purpose. It is our most important mission in government, and I look forward to working with you on it.*
>
> *Yours,*
> *Rt Hon Marjorie Wilson*

He threw his phone across the office. The piles of fish food came clattering down. She'd screwed him over again.

TANK ON THE LAWN

Parliament Square was crammed with cats making their way to work in their usual chaotic and unruly way. Half of them probably have useless jobs that are of absolutely no use to society, mused Hector. *Advisers. The world has too many self-important, good-for-nothing advisers. And directors. In charge of things like gender neutral trays.* He scoffed. *And the likes of Douglas. What a useless, wretched little tom.* Today would be the day MPs and journalists would find out what an absolute coward he was.

Hector licked moonshot off the fur on his chest and chewed on his cinnamon flavoured nip leaf. He was sitting comfortably inside the driver's hold, enjoying the fan blowing on his face. He pushed down further onto the gas and felt a chug. *What a beautiful piece of kit.* The tank was such a smooth ride and he felt safe inside, protected by the armoured plates. *Cosy. Colossal. Powerful.*

He could flatten Douglas in a second with this thing. Sixty tonnes of pure metal delivering tough diplomacy. He lay back, peering through the periscope, chuckling to himself, inching forward. Perhaps he could shove that ghastly tom inside the cannon and spit him out like a fly. Fling him all the way to Russia and let that General Bulgakov bloke deal with him. He would happily fire Douglas over the border wall and swap him for a few illegals from the Greek Islands. Maybe he could drive this beautiful gargantuan thing to Victoria and give his mansion a good bashing. Or just follow him around everywhere. Hector chuckled. *Imagine being followed around by a tank.*

Skrrr! Hector jumped. He felt himself skid as he attempted to navigate the thing around Parliament Square. He had better slow down, he didn't want to inflict any bruises. There was Jitters, zigzagging left and right, and bashing his way into commuters with his oversized rucksack. That bag of nerves always seemed to be in a rush, what was he up to? *Silly fool.* And there was Angus from *The Meowington Times*, with his camera, looking straight at him. He was looking confused for some reason. Nice to see he had turned up on time.

He took another swig from his hipflask. His control of the heavy-duty vehicle was almost flawless, it was spectacular, and now everyone inside Westminster would witness it. He'd spent all night working on his banner on the side of his tank:

TIME TO FLATTEN THE WRETCHED DOUGLAS SCHNITTY — AND MAKE BRITAIN GREAT AGAIN!

He felt a sharp juddering as he veered onto the pavement. He saw pedestrians in front of him panicking and darting in every direction. He skimmed a bunch of placards on the green. Something about sharing is caring, his blurry vision couldn't make it out. A group wearing bright coloured robes scattered out of the way. *Hippies.* He flattened a marquee and crashed into a row of iron bollards. 'Mayday… Mayday!' screamed Hector to himself, as he went flying out of his seat.

He clambered out of the tank and darted through the chaos. That had quickly unravelled into a disaster. He dodged the security at Westminster Hall, the useless Cat Eye lot, who all seemed to be running and hiding from the crash. He took his moment, climbed the side of the building, and dived into an open window. Luckily, he still had his hipflask. And his phone. He looked for Angus' number.

'Hello, hi? Are you at the tank incident in Westminster per chance?' he squealed. 'Have you seen what has happened?'

He carried on in his best catess impression, 'I am a concerned bystander… I'd rather not disclose my identity if it is all the same with you. I am very worried about Hector Perp Pahpousson *Esquire*, the Defence Secretary. I have it on good authority that it was he who was commanding the tank.'

He tried to catch his breath. 'What? No, I am not the great Hector. Sadly. But he is very badly injured, you know.'

He seemed to be in the middle of an empty library. It felt grander than the one he had had in his mansion as a kitten. 'We are in an undisclosed location,' he screeched. 'But you must inform your readers that he was wronged. By Douglas Schnitty, a wretched, snivelly little tom. This is in the public interest. Hector is in a very bad way. Let us pray for his recovery.'

The Defence Secretary hung up. He cackled loudly, his newly found high-pitched voice echoing in the high-ceilinged room. He spotted a book on the emperors of the Roman Empire and began flicking through it.

*

Douglas scrolled the headlines before his nightly swim.

THE MEOWINGTON TIMES

NEWS IN BRIEF

An anonymous briefing, suspected to originate from the heart of government, alleges that the Deputy Prime Minister has lost everything in a messy divorce and is cohabiting with a fish. It states that Douglas Schnitty is of an "unsound mind", a "Global Alliance fetishist", and that his long-suffering wife is relieved to be rid of him.

He tried to slow his breathing; his heart felt as if something was clenching at it. There was only one cat that could be behind this, that knew of the divorce. This was a low blow. He thought of how tired he was. It was times like this where he could say goodbye to it all. He could let the currents sweep him away at the river tonight. Knock back a chicken and tiger lily concoction in the morning. So many easy ways to end it. That would be some justice. After all, his darling Rara didn't get a shot at life, why should he?

It was time to leave for his nightly swim. He was late. The

best thing he could do for now would be to keep his promise to little Rara and keep swimming. Plus, it would energise him for tomorrow. Big day tomorrow, he'd be accompanying the PM to meet the Global Cats Alliance president. And this non-story would be forgotten about by then.

GRAND PALACE, FRANCE

Monsieur Claude walked precisely and delicately on the thick, cream cloth draped over his royal table. He nibbled on the long line of cheese, sausage meat, pork belly and giant shrimp. 'Putain,' — *whore*, he growled under his breath as his presidential crown kept slipping onto his nose.

'C'est incredible. And also, incredibly stupid, you coming here like this,' he said, shaking his head like a hooman. 'Unannounced and having the nerve to demand such... such —'

'You have got to work with us,' spluttered Marjorie, wearing her trademark midnight blue dress and pearl collar. 'I have an, er... well, I have an election coming up. If you help me, we may not have to do anything drastic.'

Douglas sat across the banquet staring at the two of them. This was a win-win situation for us. Get the concessions in the bag or say goodbye. Why the hell was she yielding already?

'OK, well, be realistic, oui? Tell us what you Brits really want, tell us why you have really come here.'

Marjorie looked away.

'Well? Do you even know what you want?'

'Drop the ban on our jumbo packs of fried fish skins for starters?' she muttered.

Fucking hell, thought Douglas, was she asking or demanding?

'Non. No way, that is a clear red line.'

'Monsieur Claude, listen, this is very unpopular back home. Let me be frank, you are messing with the UK's favourite snack, we will not forgive you.'

'Excusez moi, but all member states have agreed to enforce this. Besides, you benefit from this measure more than anyone else. The whole world can see that you Brits have a huge problem with obesity —'

Douglas cut him off with a hiss. How dare he insult us like that? Especially while sitting there and stuffing his face with pork belly and goujons. Global Alliance President or not, why was she letting him get away with this?

'I know this is hard to hear, and I say it as your friend, but you are known as les fatties of the Alliance. The ban on jumbo fried fish skins stays. It will literally save your lives!'

'We need movement on the fried fish skins, and you also need to lift the regulations on our nip leaves,' growled Marjorie.

'Absolutely non-negotiable! Every member state has to legally limit the nip content in their leaves.'

'No.'

'What do you mean, no?'

'We cannot have you regulating our nip leaves. Cats come from, er… well, cats come from all over the world to chew on our world class nip leaves.'

'I've already explained this to you — you can't have more than thirty per cent nip inside a leaf, this is fair for everyone.'

'Well, we Brits like to chew on the strong stuff. This is non-negotiable.'

'That's why you are so, how do you say, so high and irrational all the time.'

'And thirdly, we need exemption from the Rule of, er… well, the Rule of 18.'

Oh God, we are done for, thought Douglas. Thought she'd had enough sense to drop this stupid idea. Voters will obviously choose whoever promises them the most sleep.

'Listen, Madame Wilson, every cat needs her sleep. Even British ones, oui?'

'Well, let me be frank. Either you compromise with us now, monsieur, or we walk out of the Alliance altogether once I increase my majority at the election.' Marjorie jumped up and stormed off.

Douglas stared at the President. *Nobody even knows his name or what he does. Waste of space.* He rose and crept slowly towards Claude. 'Uh, shall we talk privately, monsieur?'

They slipped out of the window onto the roof terrace. Where the hell had she disappeared to, right at the crux of the negotiations? Well, he tried. He came with her and supported her despite her showing him again and again that she didn't give a shit about the needy. Now she had well and truly screwed it.

'Uh, listen, Claude, you didn't hear this from me, but she is all talk. As the Deputy Prime Minister, I shouldn't be telling you this, but the reality is that we are never going to leave. The Alliance is special.'

Claude raised his leg and started grooming.

Charming! 'Look, Claude, the Alliance is a big part of

who we are, we have a proud and shared history together. Truth is, we need you just as much as you need us.'

She deserves to fail, he thought. No game plan, no social skills, zero empathy. We could have gone back with serious concessions.

'If I didn't care about the Alliance and our special friendship, I wouldn't be telling you this, Claude. Stay strong. Do not give her an inch.'

'Merci, mon ami.' — *Thank you, my friend.*

'If she does not get what she wants, she will be out before the election. And a sensible, more centrist head will almost certainly take her place. Someone a lot more pro-Alliance.'

'Thank God we can rely on true friends like you. She is not living in the real world.'

*

The press were scrabbling for front row seats in the gardens of the Grand Palace, as Marjorie went through her lines.

'We must work together, ensure we work together as partners, but, er… wait, er, but have the freedom to do what is right for our own country. Those are the key messages I'd like to get across.'

'Too bland, Prime Minister,' said Douglas. She was a disaster. She messed up the negotiations. And she didn't have the guts to tell him where to go.

'Uh, you need to get out there and show them you mean business,' he continued. 'Get your teeth into the hot topics of fried fish skins and nip leaves. Tell them that we will sleep as much or as little as we want to. That sort of thing. Let out a hiss or two, threaten to walk.'

'How do you think the talks have gone?'

'As well as they could, given the circumstances. I thought you handled it brilliantly, Prime Minister.'

'I shouldn't have stormed out.'

'Don't blame you. Anyone would have done the same. Pompous git.'

'What happened after I left, Douglas?'

'Well, I told him we were dead serious, and he needed to think very carefully about whether he wants to lose us, and our membership money.'

Even if we did walk, and even if we got all those millions back, she wouldn't give a single British Mew to the slum cats. She needed to be removed, Douglas told himself. 'Look, they are calling our bluff. You must stay strong, Prime Minister. Don't give him an inch.'

'OK. Can you please take some pics of me up there? I'll try and look at you, so pay attention. I'll post them on social media later, show the public that I'm, er… well, that I am one of them.'

Utterly embarrassing, Douglas thought.

'Good morning. Bonjour.' Claude's crown slipped onto his nose. 'Grr,' he went under his breath. 'I am pleased to welcome our friend and ally, the British Prime Minister, and we have had some interesting discussions on their membership of the Global Alliance.'

'Thank you, Mr President, and thank you for your hospitality. We have had some constructive discussions over some first-class sausage meat. It was, er… *epic*, one could say.' She looked over and grinned awkwardly.

Claude looked confused. Douglas looked away. There was no way he was snapping that.

'But I must cut to the chase. We want, er... well, we want two regulations lifted immediately. First, the ban on jumbo packs of fried fish skins, and second the limit on nip inside our world-famous nip leaves —'

'Let me stop you there, Prime Minister. These rules exist for good reason. They remove any unfair trading advantage, and they are designed to improve global health and wellbeing.'

Marjorie jolted herself upright and spat out another one of her gormless smiles. There was definitely something wrong with her.

'Is everything OK, Prime Minister?' Claude enquired.

'I respectfully disagree,' she blurted out, ignoring him. 'These rules are overbearing and unnecessary. My government should decide what goes inside our nip leaves, or whether we want to outlaw, er... well, our favourite snack in jumbo size.'

'Non. Let me be clear, madame, we want you to stay with us inside the Alliance. We are better together, stronger united. But I am sorry to say we are at an impasse.'

Marjorie stormed over to President's podium and leapt up next to him.

'How about just one?' she whispered. 'Just say you will consider the matter of the jumbo fried fish skins. That will allow me to go home and say we have, er... well, made progress. We will be more likely to stay with you.'

'Non. Absolutely not. It is impossible.'

'Well, then, there is nothing left to discuss. Douglas, get

ready with your camera!' Marjorie glared at her counterpart, bit his ear, and skulked off.

'This press conference is over,' she said. 'Let's go home.'

THE RESIGNATION

Meanwhile back in London, the Defence Secretary opened the brown envelope that had been shoved under his door.

Confidential: Hector Perp Pahpousson, it read in a tiny, antlike font.

> Dear Hector,
>
>   It is with regret that I tender my resignation from my position as your press adviser. My last day of employment will be in exactly five days from now. It has certainly been an interesting learning experience working with you...
>
>   Sincerely,
>   Fee.

'Fee! Fee! Get in here. At once!'

He closed his eyes. 'Phoebe!'

The little brown and grey striped cat shuffled in with a pout on her face. 'It's Ffion, not Phoebe. And before you start —'

'Well, this is a fine how-do-you-do! Why, oh, why on earth are you leaving me?'

He wandered to the window and looked up to the moon. 'Am I not good to you? Do I not turn a blind eye when you nick my cream? I know you do, I've seen the splatterings behind your ears, you know. Have I ever said anything?'

'I'm tired, Hector —'

'Do I not do impromptu nice things for you? Remember that time I bought you your very own pair of gold pyjamas, identical to mine? Do I not educate you? Impart words of wisdom upon you? Tell you my finest jokes? Knock knock…'

'No, Hector.'

'Come on, knock knock…'

'No.'

'Knock knock…'

She looked irked. 'Who's there?'

'Interrupting cow.'

She spoke slowly. 'Interrupting cow wh —'

'Moooooh!' Delivered with spectacular timing.

'Good one, Hector,' she said reluctantly. 'But I'm not changing my mind, I'm sorry.' She looked skinny and bony.

'That's fine.' Hector started howling. 'I have treated you like my very own. I will be extremely sorry to lose you. Let's have a drink.'

'No, I really can't,' said Fee, shifting uncomfortably. 'I have to get off.'

'One,' insisted Hector. 'Just the one. If you must leave me, it's the least I can do to thank you for your very fine service.'

'OK, fine. One.'

Hector wandered over to his row of six crystal decanters and sniffed at the pale moonshot at the end.

'How about this rare number from the Lowlands?'

'Sure.'

'It is the very finest and smoothest of the lot. 500 British Mews this bottle was. Only the best for my Phoebe.'

'Ffion!'

'Apologies.'

'And anyway, I should not be talking to you, Hector.'

'Whyever not?'

'You crashed a bloody battle tank on Parliament Square! And you almost flattened the protestors at the sharing is caring thing! What were you thinking?'

'Ah yes, the hippies, I saw them. There was that one rather unfortunate incident. You know, someone definitely tampered with that thing. It was fine one minute and then —'

'And flatten Douglas Schnitty, really?'

'Ah yes. It was: *time to flatten the wretched Douglas Schnitty — and make Britain great again!*'

'But why, Hector?'

'Look, it worked. My audience right now is my Black Cat colleagues. And the media. We need a bold approach to leave the Global Alliance. And in any case, a little provocation never harmed anybody.'

Hector topped up his bowl.

'Also, I was wronged, you know. Look, Fee, I am sorry. I know I haven't made your life easy here. I know colleagues view me as a bit odd at times, a bit provocative —'

'A bit provocative? They think you're bloody cuckoo!'

'Yes perhaps. But in my defence —'

There was a scratch on the door. Hector pounced towards it and dragged a bucket inside.

'That thing's huge, Hector, what's inside?'

'Prawns.'

'Prawns?'

'Yes. Crevettes. I took the liberty of ordering us a supersize bucket of crevettes. You must be hungry.'

'A supersize bucket of crevettes?'

'Yes. Take it as a leaving present.'

He circled the bucket and dived into the crevettes. 'Come, Fee, jump in!'

Fee let out a giggle and followed him in. They spent the night munching on their giant prawns and getting through his expensive moonshot.

'Oh, Hector, you are infuriating but you can be so bloody charming.'

'Well, yes. I mean perhaps. Would you like me to tell you a secret?'

'Oh God.'

'The tank was only the start. I know a thing or two about Douglas, and soon it will be plastered all over the front pages of the national news. We will expose his sorry little secret past —'

'No.'

'And that, my dear, will be the final nail in his coffin.'

'Oh, Hector, no.' Fee scowled at him.

'But shh, you mustn't tell a soul.'

*

Hector plonked himself next to his cream fountain. It was 5am and Fee had left a while back, giving him a long kiss on the lips. It was most uncharacteristic of her. He poured himself another moonshot on the rocks. He stroked the photo of himself standing to attention in crisp army uniform. He was so much leaner back then. Oh, how he longed for those days again. Popular with the lads and sought after by the she-cats. He was a catch. He looked dashing in his uniform, so svelte.

He hoisted himself up and fell backwards into the fountain of cream. He eventually dragged himself out and reached the letter in his desk. He attempted to unfold the delicate thing, covering it in drips of cream. *The decision has been made to terminate your employment for reason of misconduct*, said the blurry, black writing. He shoved it back in the drawer. Why did it have to end that way? He was such a natural. Well respected and admired for his shock action tactics. He let out a soft yowl.

A little flicker of light caught his eye as he was drifting off. He noticed two bright dots behind the coat rack. They went out in a fraction of a second. What the hell was that? They were like lasers pointing at him.

'By golly! I am being assassinated!' he shouted. 'Hello?'

All was still. 'Who's there? Come out! Reveal yourself!'

Nothing. He crept behind the curtain. 'Hello? Are you a certain Phoebe who has left me with a heavy heart?'

Silence. *Must be going mad. Maybe what they say is true. I blame the moonshot. It's making me see things.*

*

PM'S ELECTION GAMBLE PAYING OFF, BUT PUBLIC CALL DEPUTY A "TRAITOR"

By Angus, Political Correspondent,
The Meowington Times

An exclusive poll, conducted by Catopinions for The Meowington Times, shows Marjorie Wilson's lead has dropped by eight points over the last week. It puts her on 38%, compared to 30% for the leader of the Cats Collective. The shift comes on the back of the frosty Global Alliance meeting in Paris earlier this week, in which she failed to secure a single concession. However, two-thirds of the 5,000 cats polled, said they admired her brave leadership and willingness to stand up for the country. Exactly half of respondents also back her cuts programme, and agreed with statements such as "she is doing the tough but right thing" and "she is putting the country first".

A perhaps surprising 45% said they would like Hector Perp Pahpousson to become Deputy Leader, describing him as "honest" and "likeable." This is a dramatic turnaround in the fortunes of the Defence Secretary, who just a few weeks ago was disregarded by many as "a bit of a joker".

However, the poll makes dire reading for the current Deputy, Douglas Schnitty. Just 11% think he is doing a good job. More than a third suspect he is closely associated with the Global Alliance, and a whopping seven in ten say he is a "traitor" for having betrayed the Defence Secretary, demonstrating that Hector's antics seem to be sticking with the public.

An anonymous government source said, "Schnitty is finished. One has to wonder whether he is even a Freedom Cat. Marjorie would have given that crackpot the boot by now if we weren't three weeks away from a general election."

So many ways to end the misery, thought Douglas. It could all be over tonight. No. He wasn't going to go down that path again. He had to keep going, keep his head up. He had a bigger calling. And his darling Rara had his back.

He headed out for his nightly swim. It would keep him sane. And in any case, the Defence Secretary would soon get his comeuppance.

THE MIDNIGHT
MOON DANCE

Hector was reclining in the London Stadium, snug in his white silk robe. He felt superior. Spiritual. Immortal even. It was the annual Midnight Moon Dance and the stadium was filling fast. Tickets had sold out within seconds once again, it was just as well the organisers considered him as a cat of serious social standing. He was after all quite the furore these days.

This was the gathering of the year, he'd been looking forward to bumping heads with the elite for weeks. He spotted poets and fashion directors, actors, Olympic hunters, and ballerinas in the stalls. The moggy Prime Minister and her merry band of bores were nowhere to be seen. *Pahahah!*

The spectacular live piano performance of Beethoven's *Moonlight Sonata* was drowning out the distant screams of "no more cuts" and "resign, Prime Minister!" Ah, speaking of her, there she was. Curled up in the bloody VIP box. Where he should have been. They were clearly letting any Tom, Dick or Moggy in these days. You couldn't miss her with her pink collar and matching ballet shoes. *I pity her, sitting on her lonesome.*

Big Ben started bonging in the distance. It was midnight. Hector joined the crowd onto their hind legs. He was ready for the customary yowling ceremony under the bright moonlight. The siren-like yowls grew louder and more intense. He admired the echo they were making. They were probably being heard across the Capital.

The first dancer leapt onto the stage. She looked beautiful. Her dainty nose and fluffy tail reminded him of Glenda, his first love. She was such a sweetheart, and she had the most seductive legs. Imagine if it had all worked out in the army, they probably would have wed, had the most beautiful kittens by now. He would have become General. Perhaps she would be lying next to him at the Midnight Moon Dance. Life surely would have been different. Instead, she cruelly cut off all contact with him after his promising career ended so abruptly. *It's sad how quickly we move on from the ones we love,* he mused.

He saw the big-eared oaf, Douglas, approach the Prime Minister. *The weasel who climbs up the greasy pole. Well, he should enjoy it while it lasts.* And sitting behind them was that nodding tom Jitters, and his mother next to him. *What would he do without his dear old mother?*

The yowling ceremony broke into rapturous applause and Mads, a beautiful sandy Norwegian Forest Cat, began the first dance to a Mozart number.

'Ah *Die Zauberflote*,' said Hector. '*The Magic Flute.* The Queen of the Night persuades the Prince to rescue her daughter from captivity.' Hector turned to see whether his favourite journalist was impressed.

'Look, Angus, we need to talk about Mr Deputy Prime Minister over there. Not out of any spite or malice, but because the truth about him needs to be heard. It is in the public interest.'

'Ah, yes, what's going on with you both? I got a very strange phone call by the way. You were on your death bed, apparently, after your tank stunt. I understand you wanted to flatten him?'

'Well, I survived. Thanks for asking.'

'Is this about your leadership ambitions?'

'What? My only ambition is for our troops, our security, our glorious —'

'But you are making moves? You've got close to 80 MPs behind a potential leadership bid, have you not?'

'Look, there is probably more chance of big-eared Douglas over there being catapulted into Siberia.'

'So, it is true that —'

'But speaking of that wretch, did you know he had a daughter called Rara? And do you know what happened to her? She's dead. You should ask him what happened. Why his wife *really* left him.'

Hector watched Mads the ballerina as she made her way around the stage in a slow and delicate horse-like gallop. He rose to his feet and meowed excitedly as she performed a special shuffle, crossing her forelegs perfectly over each other.

'Bravo! Spectacular! Listen, Angus, would you do your beloved Defence Secretary a favour?'

'Sure, what do you need?'

'Speaking of Douglas and his ex, Tamara —'

'Tamara? What about her?'

'You must know where she lives, I beg of you to give me her address.'

'What? Why do you need her address, Hector?'

'I need to settle some unfinished business.'

'No, Hector.'

Mads leapt suddenly, her long and stretched out body gliding gracefully through the air. Like a superhero.

'Sir! I promise not to harm her. I just want to… to borrow her for a few days. To send a message.'

'Um…'

'I won't lay a single claw on her, promise.'

'No, Hector. I will pretend this conversation never happened.'

The stadium went wild as Mads landed back on earth in her white socks, bowed, and soaked up the adulation with a silent meow.

*

'That ballerina was incredible, Mads! She was flying even higher than my poll ratings.' Marjorie chuckled.

'Yes, indeed she was, Prime Minister,' said Douglas. He was studying her carefully but needed to be less obvious about it.

'Must say you looked phenomenal last night,' he said with a straight face. 'Your, uh, pink ballet shoes sparkled in the moonlight.'

'Thank you, I still practise when I can. I was county champion back in the day. By the way, did you see that Hector in the stalls? He was whispering away to that *Meowington Times* journalist. Wonder what he is concocting now.'

'Forget about him, he's irrelevant. A busted flush.'

Douglas watched on as the Prime Minister picked at her fish gravy supper. He couldn't forget that she'd totally played him over the 50 million funding for the so-called forgotten national priorities. If she won this election, thousands more would become homeless. He'd just read the *Institute of Cat Affairs* report which forecast that the number of homeless living in the bins would reach a million by this time next year, and 1.5 million by next Christmas. And they were a reputable outfit, usually on the money with their forecasts.

'You know, you need to, uh, push yourself further, get yourself out there a bit more.'

'How, er… well, how exactly do you mean?'

'Well, you are indeed doing well in the polls. But you really should be aiming for a landslide victory this time. Maybe you should push your cuts agenda harder, be more daring. Talk to those who are not your natural voters.'

'I'm not sure about that, Douglas, why rock the ship?'

'Because you can win them around. You know, you should consider making an appearance on *Sunday Questions*, you'd be the first Freedom Cat Prime Minister to ever go on that programme.'

'That's a bad idea. It's a biased programme, and those lefties would never vote for me in, er… in a million years. Why would I bother?'

'Because you are strong. You can appeal to a much wider audience, get your message across. That's how you'll get your big victory.'

'I don't know, Douglas. It's a big risk, so close to the election.'

'Exactly, we are coming up to the big day. It is your opportunity to push your cuts, explain why they are the morally right thing to do. Talk about the impossible Global Cats Alliance conundrum you are facing. Win them over, and you're guaranteed a landslide.'

Marjorie's eyes lit up. 'You can be so persuasive. Do you really think I can do it?'

Douglas took her paw. 'I have every faith in you, Prime Minister.'

It was time to force her onto the public. The more they got to see of her, the more they would come to loathe her. The quicker she'd be gone.

'Oh, my, Douglas, your paws are so soft!'

'Uh, thanks, I moisturise daily,' he muttered.

'They are, er... well, they are kitten soft.'

Douglas pretended he needed to scratch his ear and pulled away. 'Tell you what, Prime Minister, let me take care of the arrangements. Let's do it next Sunday, no time to waste. All you need to worry about is which collar you'll wear.'

'I have just the one in mind.'

'Good. And then strut into that studio, and win the argument. Just be your magnificent self. Now excuse me for just a minute.'

Douglas snuck into the bathroom and whipped out his burner phone. He kept the door slightly ajar and loudly patted his paws on the wood litter.

Comrades, the Prime Minister will be appearing on Sunday Questions next week. There are still many free seats left. This is your chance to fill out the audience and hold her to account. Expose her on live television and make sure that poll lead of hers evaporates. Mobilise your supporters. Tell them to get booking asap. Your anonymous friend.

The stench of her cheap air freshener made him retch. It was time to leave.

MESSAGE FROM
THE HEAVENS

Up in the air, Hector looked back at his reflection. His sharp teeth were on full display. He had managed to pull off the loop de loop marvellously. *Gulp!* He took a swig from his hipflask. His beloved hipflask, always accompanying him on life's great adventures.

It was the last Thursday of the month and the Westminster food market, popular with MPs, looked busy down below. He was missing his monthly sampling of exotic street foods, rustled up by some of the finest chefs in the country. He drooled at the thought of the huge meaty scotch eggs with the bright yellow yolks, and the seafood paella with the jumbo prawns. He scowled at the thought of missing out on the freshly fried fish skins, which the antagonists at the Global Alliance wanted to ban.

No matter, it would be a worthwhile sacrifice. No doubt the whole of Westminster would be watching, transfixed, wowed by his performance. And they would soon get his note loud and clear from the heavens.

He had chosen the red propeller plane with the big wings for his mission. *Rarrr! Rarrr!* He held his breath as he darted across the skies. He turned upside down and looped beautifully, taking care to spell out the letters with precision.

HOT 4 HEC
DOUG IS A...

He was a skilled pilot, one-of-a-kind, revered by friend and foe. Maybe he would get himself one of these beauties. Just imagine the fun. He could fly Douglas out of the country, on a one-way ticket. Over the border wall. Dangle him from the skies, cut the rope and wave him off as he descends into the Channel. Or perhaps Mr Deputy Prime Minister would like to be awoken in his mansion, awoken by a plane accidently crash landing into his dreams.

He stopped chuckling and froze as he heard the engine chug. It was an unwelcome chug. It sounded as if it was misfiring. Losing power. He peeked at the gauges below, they were in the red. He attempted to give it some throttle, but the plane seemed to be dying slowly. 'Maaay-daaaay!'

The damn thing started popping and spluttering loudly as it bobbed up and down. It was making him nauseous. He retched as it started to spin, the stream of tuna-scented vomit flying everywhere. He had no choice but to abandon his sentence in the clouds. He looked out of the window and made out Westminster Bridge getting bigger.

'Abort, abort!' he screamed at himself as he descended fast towards the river. He took his chance and lunged out of the plane. He grappled onto the cord and gave it a tug. *Whoosh!* The bright yellow parachute sprang into life. The gathering below was fixated, the stunned faces coming into focus. 'Sabo-taaaage!' he screamed at them. The grey smoke from below swept over him. Two fighter jets rushed towards the red ruins in the water.

A VISIT FROM THE
BLACK CATS

Douglas was stuffing velvety cheese into the mouse, making a right mess of it. He'd caught it overnight in honour of his darling Rara. It was the first anniversary of her passing and cheesy stuffed mouse had been her favourite meal in the whole world. He felt anxious for some reason; he had a lot on his mind, a lot to discuss with Rara. She would give him clarity. He couldn't believe it had been a year. The sight of her struggling against the current, her desperate squeals, the water slowly taking away her scent. It would be etched in his memory forever. He would never forget that feeling of loss. Of finality. Of deep self-loathing.

There was a soft scratch on the door.

'May we come in, Douglas?'

Four black cats filed in before he could answer. He'd recognised them from the Society meetings; they were senior, not to be messed with. They certainly weren't here for laughs.

'We are a delegation from the Black Cats Society, we're here to deliver you an extremely important letter.'

'Uh, who from?'

'All will become crystal clear as soon as you open it.'

'Uh, OK...'

One of the group snapped a picture of the envelope in Douglas' paws and mumbled something about proof of receipt.

'And I would like to offer you some wise counsel,' continued the one at the front. 'It will be best if you take heed of the contents and act in a timely manner. Don't make things any worse for yourself.'

The four black cats marched out in a line.

> *Dear Douglas,*
>
> *We the undersigned request that you stand down from your role as Deputy Prime Minister immediately. We have evidence that suggests you sympathise with the Global Alliance, and we believe you are considering crossing the floor immediately. You have acted dishonourably in your treatment of our Defence Secretary and we think you have many questions to answer about your private life, which are in the public interest. As such, we have lost confidence in you. A copy of this letter has been sent to The Meowington Times.*

It had the pawprint of one Hector Perp Pahpousson and 103 MPs. He'd played a blinder; unpick the Deputy, and the PM would soon follow. Having 103 MPs turn against you, a third of the Party, was lethal.

He hadn't expected such a big backlash. How could the Party not see through the demented Defence Secretary? Maybe he didn't belong in the Freedom Cats after all. Maybe the Party he knew and loved was long gone. Maybe he should resign. It could all be over this time tomorrow, if he wanted it to be. He was tired.

FOODSTAMPS

'She-cats and toms, the Prime Minister of the United Kingdom!' A dazzling spotlight fell onto the plump, grey British Blue as he swaggered onto the stage. The crowd went wild. His huge gunmetal aviators covered his round, grey face. He stared into the arena where fans were clambering over themselves to catch a glimpse. He acknowledged his ma at the front and looked over at Ffion. She was standing beside him in her beautiful white dress, she gave him a slow blink. He touched her ear with his lips, and whispered he loved her. 'Prrr,' she replied. 'I love you more.'

He strode slowly up to the microphone. Two she-cats at the front were reaching out trying to touch his soft, grey hair. He soaked up the atmosphere, the adoration, the stardom.

'Thank you. I am truly humbled. A big victory.'

The stadium went wild.

'Thank you for backing me, for giving me your vote. I promise to respect and honour the biggest prize in the land. That of Britain's sexiest MP.'

'Ji-tters! Ji-tters!' chanted the crowd.

'And I want to thank my darling ma. She's in the crowd, stand up ma. I love you dearly.'

'We have our Ji-tters! We love our Ji-tters!' they shouted.

'And I want to thank the love of my life.' He gazed lovingly at Ffion. She purred in his ear.

Jitters dived off the stage and into the crowd, bumping heads and signing baseball caps. 'I have a poster of you in my bedroom,' said a little she-cat.

This was the happiest day of his life. It ended abruptly with a loud knock on the door.

'Come in!'

'Wow, you look great,' said the camera cat.

Back in his office after an eventful lunch hour, the Minister for Welfare and General Sums had changed into a crisp white shirt and a red necktie with white polka dots. The Prime Minister was making the final tweaks to her manifesto. She was resisting his brainchild on food stamps for some reason. He would make a fantastic video to persuade her, put some soft pressure on her. Besides, this was the moment to make his big entrance onto social media. Show off his loving personality, his bright ideas. It was time to build his fanbase.

'You need a better background than just a plain white wall,' said the camera cat. 'Why don't you lie on top of your desk?'

'It l-l-looks too m-m-messy.'

'Don't worry about that, it shows you're busy.'

Jitters took the groceries out of his shopping bag and carefully began organising them on his desk. 'Can you see a-a-all these?' he asked.

'Yep, perfect — can see them clearly. But you need to relax a bit. Your ears look all tense and pointed. And your back is hunched. You look like you're about to attack your viewer. Relax!'

'S-s-s-sorry.'

'OK and rolling now, from the top, whenever you're ready.'

Jitters froze. 'Is… Is my angle right? D-D-Do I look a bit too well-fed from this s-s-side?'

'No, you look great.'

'OK… Today I want to t-t-t-talk to you about —'

'Hang on, need to hit record again.'

'S-s-sorry.'

'OK. 3… 2… 1… and rolling!'

'T-T-Today I want to t-t-talk to you about w-w-welfare reform and how f-f-food stamps will make the system fairer for all. It may sound c-c-controversial, but food stamps will ensure money is spent on p-p-proper food and eating more h-h-healthily.'

Krrr krrr. There was a scratch on the door.

'Oh s-s-sorry. Come in.'

It was Douglas.

'Hi, Douglas, I'm just recording a v-v-video for my social m-m-media.'

'Uh, no problem, I can wait.' He lay out of shot.

Jitters slow blinked into the camera. 'We too often gorge on greasy f-f-f-fast food such as f-f-f-fried chicken and f-f-frozen mouse tails. We are g-g-getting fatter because of it. B-B-But I've done my r-r-research and for the same p-p-price as a fried chicken meal f-f-for a family of five, I managed to b-b-buy this big bag of rice, this t-t-tuna, two d-d-dozen eggs, some kippers —'

'Stop… Stop. Sorry to interrupt you in your flow, Jitters, but when you said kippers, you pointed at the tuna. And when you were talking about the tuna, you pointed at the eggs. It got a bit confusing. You need to point at the item you are talking about.'

'Sorry. My mind is a bit d-d-distracted.' He hadn't expected an audience. Ffion also needed to see this somehow. She'd come running back in a heartbeat once she found out he was a social media influencer.

'OK, let's go and remember to relax, keep it natural!'

'So... so to c-c-c-conclude, I can reveal exclusively t-t-to you that I will be asking the P-P-Prime Minister to replace a significant proportion of benefit m-m-money with f-f-food stamps. It will mean less money spent on n-n-nip leaf and moonshot, it will mean e-e-enough food on your table and healthier f-f-food. And if we all eat h-h-healthier, we will have more energy and we'll feel b-b-better. Which will save our health system money in the long run. Th-Th-Thank you.'

Jitters continued staring intensely into the camera. He slow blinked again. He had just set up his profile on PawPad, and he was excited to see how his very first video would perform. *Maybe I should film mini videos on how to cook healthy meals on a budget. Week one could be pan fried mackerel and beetroot. Or kippers and poached egg. We could call it "Dinner with Jitters". Ma could be my special guest...*

'Uh, well done, Jitters,' said Douglas. 'Listen, did you know about this letter of no confidence in me?'

'Y-Y-Yes. I refused to s-s-sign it.'

'Did he ask you to?'

'Y-Y-Yes. I'd come t-t-to inform you the other night but you weren't i-i-in, and I didn't want to put it in writing, leave a t-t-trail. S-S-Sorry.'

'Don't worry, Jitters.'

Good old Jitters, Douglas thought. Head down, working hard, seeing right through the Hector bandwagon.

SUNDAY QUESTIONS

'Let's now welcome Prime Minister Marjorie Wilson onto the programme. You are the first Freedom Cat leader to ever join us.'

Marjorie hopped onto the guest sofa and reclined. She glared at the audience as they booed and hissed.

Douglas was prowling behind the scenes. The "Stop the Cuts" coalition seemed to have turned out in full force, as did the Public Workers Union. *Good. That lot mean business. They will literally chop her up into pieces. Serve her up on a platter.*

'Prime Minister, why have you called an election so soon into your term?'

Marjorie squinted as the studio spotlight turned to point in her face. 'Well, good morning and thank you, er… well, thank you for having me. Listen, I do not want this election any more than you do. But sadly, I have been pushed into a corner. Our public finances are out of control, and I am making sure we do the right thing to remedy —'

'Your cuts are nuffink but ideological!' screamed a she-cat in the audience.

'What would you do instead?' Marjorie was quick to shut her down. 'The last government pretty much bankrupted us. I will give the economy, er… well, the strong medicine it needs.'

'Yeah, but we don't want your medicine! You are decimating our public services!'

'Well, a bankrupt country will not be able to afford any public services full stop!'

She was on a roll, holding her own so far. Douglas scanned the audience. Half of them were snoozing; they needed to wake up, ratchet up the pressure. It would be the only way to get rid of her and end the suffering.

'What are you all about, Prime Minister?' asked the presenter. 'What exactly do you believe in?'

'Making the poor suffer!' came a shriek from the audience. 'She's forgotten her moggy roots!'

'No. I know how difficult it is. I was raised by my dear single mother in social housing on a tree estate, it was tough for us.' She paused. 'One could say, I'm from, er… from *them ends*.'

She paused some more. The audience groaned.

'But let me be frank, we need to remember who we are. Cats. We look out for ourselves and our families first and foremost. That runs in the very fibre of who we are —'

'We need to evolve,' shouted a broad chested tom. 'Move on from individualism!'

'And end up like the hoomans did fifty years ago?' growled Marjorie.

'Come off it, you know the hoomans vanished cos they were weak; they didn't know how to hunt, they had no killer instinct —'

'Let me be frank —'

'They didn't even have claws!'

'Let me be frank, the hoomans are no longer with us because, er... well, because of their failed collective ways.'

'Rubbish,' shouted the tom. 'Collectivism had nothing to do with it, you nutjob!'

'OK, let's keep it civil in the audience please,' said the presenter who seemed to have a permanent surprised look on her face. 'Prime Minister, what happened in your meeting with the Global Cats Alliance?'

'They sent her packing, innit!'

Douglas watched the audience. This was fast becoming a damp squid. We needed a bombshell moment.

'The thing is, er... well, many citizens think the Alliance is overbearing with its regulations on things like our jumbo fried fish skins and nip leaf. And forcing us to sleep for 18 hours a day.'

'Well, talk to them, then. Work it out with them, innit. You better not just pull us out!' The heckling sounded as if it was coming from the same one or two members of the audience.

'Yeah! And you better leave our sleep alone!'

'I am trying to negotiate with them,' said Marjorie, softly. 'But I must say they, they are being rather pig headed. I will always do what is right for the country.'

A stocky cat walked up on stage. 'What about all the trade, all them jobs and grants and things that we get from the Alliance, you silly cow?'

'Excuse me, I am not a cow, I am a cat.'

Marjorie yelped as a claw landed across her face. She batted the she-cat away with her paw.

'OK, no scuffles!' shouted the presenter. 'That's the end of the interview, everybody sit down!'

The show's social media correspondent entered on stage, and the cameras turned to a graphic with wavy green and red lines.

'We've been tracking real-time public reaction during this interview,' she said fiddling with her spectacles, 'and I must say, it's gone in the Prime Minister's favour. Out of a sample of 2,000 viewers, 65% say she comes across as steely and gutsy. Just over half say they are considering voting her back in.'

Marjorie was beaming away, her pointy, whitened teeth on full display. The hisses in the studio got louder.

'We also live streamed the full interview on PawPad and the Prime Minister got 1.2 thousand licks compared to just 450 bites.'

'Fucking disaster,' muttered Douglas. He slipped out of the back door of the studio.

HERO

That evening, Douglas weaved in and out of a cluster of bins. He dodged the raggedy clothes hanging to dry between them. He was back on his old turf. He had some news for his crazy she-cat friend, she was finally getting out of the slum and into a tree cabin of her own. It was on the first branch of a beautiful and vast tree close to the river. Lots of shade too. He was over the moon for her.

He passed his old patch, a moggy family was fast asleep on it. The kittens had decorated the bins with rainbows and hearts. No sign of his old neighbour. He took out some biscuits he'd packed for her and gave her bin a scratch. A beautiful, much younger, she-cat appeared.

'Uh, hello, I have come to see the elderly cat that lives here. She knows me, we used to be neighbours.'

She introduced herself as one of the nieces, her dear aunt had just passed away yesterday, it was from suspected hunger and malnutrition. Douglas felt as if his soul had been crushed. He sat down and tried to slow his erratic breathing. He couldn't howl in front of the niece; he tried to focus himself on his immaculate claws.

They'd found the body riddled with flies inside a bin, she said, offering him a bowl of water. It had weighed less than two kilograms. Douglas lay next to the mourning niece for a good hour, learning about her aunt's successful career as a spy.

'So, what happened?' Douglas asked. He was dreading whatever was about to come next.

The job had taken a toll on her mental health, she told him. She lost her life savings in a scam on the internet, and she eventually ended up in the slums.

He whispered his condolences, gave her the biscuits, and went on his way to find his kitten friend. He approached a frail feline sniffing around outside their patch.

'Excuse me, my name is Douglas Schnitty, I —'

'I know who you are,' she replied gently. 'You taught my son to hunt when he was little, you are a good soul.'

'Is he around? I'd love to say hi.'

She looked away. She had been sniffing around for hours, looking for him. She eventually admitted that he often disappeared for long periods, skipping school and getting into trouble for anti-social behaviour. Fighting and vandalism mainly. He'd been arrested twice. She started crying.

'I, uh, may have a cabin in a tree for your family.'

Her eyes lit up. It was clear that the youngster needed to be removed from the downward spiral. He told her to give him a couple of days and took off.

He headed towards some cats by the fire. They seemed to be shoving each other out of the way, watching something on a clapped-out old television.

'What an absolute hero!' one of them announced.

'Uh, excuse me, my name is Douglas Schnitty —'

'Shh,' came the collective response.

'Hector's on the telly!'

'Uh, Perp Pahpousson?' asked Douglas.

'Yah!' chimed the gathering.

Blimey, they were even speaking like him. Douglas crawled on his belly through the 40-strong crowd. The tubby black Chinchilla mix was giving an interview about some plan of his for jobs.

'Yahhp, yahhp, there would be no hunger and zero slums under my great jobs plan,' he declared. 'The homeless would live like kings and queens and they would have the most worthwhile job going — protecting our fine country. Rule Britannia!'

'Rule Britannia!' the slum cats chanted back.

'Uh, can someone fill me in here?'

'Yeah, mate,' said one of the big fellows. He looked like the slum leader. 'Hector was on the telly saying he has a plan to give us all jobs as soldiers and construction workers for his border wall.'

'That's right,' said a she-cat next to him. 'He'd pay us well and exempt us from tax. Says we'd be rich and that slums would become history.'

'Uh, OK.'

'He mentioned you and all,' said someone. 'Said you're a traitor, and that you have no ideas. Said you need to resign.'

'OK, whatever, but did he explain how he would be able to afford this grand plan of his? Especially when we are nearly bankrupt?'

'At least he's got a plan, mate,' said the big guy, stepping forward. 'What's your plan?'

'Yeah, what's your plan?' echoed the crowd.

'It's all bluff and bluster,' said Douglas. 'Don't fall for it.'

'He cares for us, mate, that's all that matters.'

'I-I doubt he has ever visited a slum in-in-in his life,' Douglas spluttered. 'I've actually *lived* in this slum. I know what it's like. I'm-I'm on your side.' He looked around and saw posters of the Defence Secretary plastered on every bin.

'Nah, mate, we'd be better off with him.'

'That's right,' interjected the she-cat beside him. 'He says you're not even a Freedom Cat. You're an FCINO!'

'What the hell is that?'

'Freedom Cat In Name Only!'

The mob had grown. 'F-CINO! F-CINO!' they chanted. Their claws were on display.

Douglas crept backwards. 'He-He'll let you down, I'm telling you.'

'Get out of our slum, you're not welcome here,' hissed the leader.

BRING DOWN
THE ZEALOT!

It was 3am in Parliament Square and Hector was staring lovingly at the classy opera singer in the flowy red dress. She was belting out an a capella rendition of *Haberna (L'amour est un oiseau rebelle)*. Her powerful voice seemed to be giving life to the bonfire behind her.

It was a good turn out, and fellow MPs and members of the press were marvelling as she floated through the audience. There was Angus with his camera out. And Jitters, looking down in the dumps. Probably because he was without his mother for once. It was time to burst Douglas' bubble once and for all, time for comeuppance.

'Fellow colleagues and citizens — what a barnstorming performance that was! I myself couldn't help but cry... cry tears of sadness and joy. I felt the raw passion in every word. L'amour est un oiseau rebelle — love is indeed a rebellious bird that none of us can tame.'

Hector trotted onto centre stage after giving a peck on the lips to the performer. He felt dapper in his black tuxedo. He gesticulated wildly, the square was fixated on him

'And it is indeed because of *my* rebellious love for *you*, a love that cannot be tamed, that I welcome you as VIPs to my fundraiser on this fine, starry night. You will get to take a shot at a common enemy of ours, and all proceeds will go towards a very good cause. A big battle bus which will be used to campaign to leave the corrupt Global Alliance!'

The audience watched the fire roaring skywards, purring enthusiastically. It looked furious, much like that weasel would be when learnt of the gathering.

The Defence Secretary unveiled a giant portrait of a black, big eared, Cornish Rex with ginger patterns on his neck and chest. 'I might have, er, borrowed this from the corridors of Parliament.' He erected it in front of the fire.

'I must inform you that this entitled tom, looking down at you with his big eyes and goofy smile, is a fraud! He is useless, he is harbouring a dark secret, which you will read about very soon, he is a… a Global Alliance lackey.'

The crowd arched their backs and hissed. He certainly knew how to get them going.

'And now, for a mere 50 of your finest British Mews, you can take a shot at Mr Deputy Prime Minister. The one who hits his left eye perfectly gets a whole year's supply of the finest double cream in the land. Made by yours truly in my very own Parliamentary office! Now, remember, focus is key. Let's bring down the zealot!'

Hector sniffed at the cold hard cash being shoved in his face. He felt the love as they chanted his name. 'Hec-tor! Hec-tor!' His shock tactics were working; he was becoming firmly positioned amongst his colleagues and the in press as the saviour of the country. And that weasel Deputy Prime

Minister was done for. He would soon go the same way as the feeble hoomans.

Hector spat on his pistol and polished it on his fur to rapturous applause. He felt the snuggly warmth of the bonfire on his back. *Kaboom!* A loud explosion sent him diving under a nearby bench. He peeked round to see the orange and yellow flames popping angrily, raging out of control. They were spreading across the square. He legged it, dodging the hundreds of cats running around aimlessly and colliding into each other.

'Oh shit,' cried Hector. 'The benches... they're bloody wooden! Mayday! MAYDAY!'

Nee-naw, nee-naw! The fire trucks scrambled onto the scene, thank goodness. They drowned out the crazed shrieking and the pop, pop, popping of the fire. He tried to hide.

TIME TO PUT THINGS RIGHT.

A few miles away on the riverbank in Putney, Douglas sobbed under the moonlight. 'Happy birthday, my darling.' He lay a bouquet of white roses for his daughter at their special spot.

'You know, I miss you every day, Rara. It doesn't get any easier.'

He arranged the petals. 'I don't know if you saw me the other night, I managed to swim a mile. Without stopping once. That was for you.'

He looked up at the bright sky. 'I'm sorry I couldn't get to you, Rara. I detest myself for it.' His tail started quivering.

'Have you seen that I've been promoted to Deputy Prime Minister? Yep, that's right, your daddy is now the second in command! Maybe you'd be a little proud of me in normal circumstances. But I need to… I need to tell you something else, my little Rara.'

He looked away. 'I did a bad thing the other day, I know you will have seen it. I stitched up the Prime Minister on *Sunday Questions*. I don't know what came over me.'

He felt heavy. 'But you know, she got scratched badly by

this thug. It just about missed her eye, thank goodness. It was my fault.'

He lay on their special spot, brushing the dirt away with his tail. 'I mean, what the hell is wrong with me? There are some things you just do not do. That's the difference between me and Hector. He's a dangerous lunatic, I should be better.'

He got up and circled round. 'I set her up to fail in Paris as well. I mean, I feel sick just thinking about what her cuts are doing to the needy and the homeless. But at least she's doing something to sort out this mess. She's gutsy, I'll give her that.'

She sure as hell was a gusty leader, he thought. Would he do any better in her position? Would the country honestly be better off if he was PM? Could he even hack the top job?

He began to wail softly. 'Your daddy knows he must do better, become a better cat. Help me, Rara. Watch over me. Help me before it's too late.'

The tide was coming in. He could end it all right now if he wanted to. Join his beloved daughter up there. Maybe he could then explain himself face to face. Douglas wailed and wailed, and eventually he fell into a deep sleep.

*

Time to put things right, thought Douglas. The election is just a week away; the leader needs me. No more games. He snuck into the Prime Minister's study.

'You are six hours late! What happened?'

'I'm sorry, Prime Minister, I, uh, had something urgent come up.'

'Never mind, I need your help with putting together the final arrangements for my, er… night of canvassing.'

'Uh, sure. What do you have in mind?' She had put her trust in him, made him her deputy, now it was time to repay her.

'I want to go into the tree estates. In the parts of London that we need to win. Camden, Islington, Southwark, Greenwich, Battersea — you know, the places we always fail in. Not this time, we can take them all if we use our resources wisely.'

'We must be careful, Prime Minister. The London estates don't like us. Why don't I take you to some of the slums in my constituency? You can talk to the homeless, it will be safer too.'

'Thanks, but I would prefer the tree estates. I am one of them, remember? Just like *Sunday Questions* the other week, I will be the first Freedom Cat Prime Minister to scratch on their cabins and really, er… well, listen to them.'

Douglas winced. He did not like this one bit. The mood out there was angry, and it would fall on him to protect her. 'Sure, when are we doing this?'

'Not we, Douglas. *I* am doing this.'

'Pardon?'

'I am doing this. Alone. It's better that way.'

'Not a good idea, Prime Minister. It's not safe for you. Safety in numbers and —'

'It will be fine,' she retorted. 'My polls are looking good. My messaging is cutting through. Look at what happened on *Sunday Questions*. Despite what the naysayers said.'

'OK, fine, but let me come with you at least.'

'Don't take this the wrong way, Douglas, but the public like me.' She started rabbiting on about understanding the public's priorities, having the right argument. 'Aren't you relieved we didn't let the slum situation distract us, er… well, throw us off course?' she said smirking away.

He was doing everything in his power not to claw her face to shreds.

'We need this election to be about Marjorie Wilson first and foremost, then the Freedom Cats. Marjorie Wilson and her Freedom Cats. Prrr, what do you think?'

The Deputy Prime Minister scowled and lowered his tail. *Someone's getting too big for her boots. Rookie error.*

'Prime Minister, I really think that —'

'Enough, Douglas, I am going it alone.'

'As you wish. Let me know which night. Oh, and leave the arrangements to me.'

'Thank you. Thursday night.'

He got up, feeling tense. *Must be loyal. A Deputy must be loyal. Need to make it up to her. But… But there's only so much one can do.* 'Excuse me for a moment.'

He locked the bathroom door behind him and started digging loudly into the premium wood litter. He began typing on his burner phone.

> *Heads up. The Prime Minister is planning a night of canvassing this Thursday. She will be in Battersea at 1am. Comrades, this will be your final opportunity to end her chances of election victory. Confront her, expose her, bring your cameras and stick it all over PawPad. Do what you must to stop her. Good luck. Your anonymous friend.*

The litter was everywhere. He stared at the message. *This is madness, best to delete it.* Twenty minutes passed. He stared some more. *Too late, I tried my best with her. She didn't listen. This is for the so-called distraction that is the homeless.* He hit send.

MOOD ON THE DOORSTEP

'Nah, not gonna bother voting dis time.'

'Oh, that's a shame, may I ask why?'

'Ah, come on, yous all da same. Nothing ever changes, duzzit? Don't matter who's in charge.'

'Listen here, I am very much different.' The Prime Minister was getting testy. 'Would you at least care to read my manifesto?'

She backed off at the sharp hiss. One of many hisses directed at her that night. Douglas hid out of sight. It was pouring with rain and Marjorie must have climbed almost sixty trees, visited hundreds of cabins. She'd been called all sorts but seemed to be taking it on the chin. Still, it must hurt.

She called for the fifth time at the branch above. There was some movement in the cabin. 'Hello? It's the Prime Minister, you can call me Marjorie. Or Marj if you prefer.' She straightened her collar. 'I just want to talk to you about the election. At least spare me two minutes. I'm just an, er… an ordinary cat. Like you.'

'Oy, piss off!' came a shout from the next tree. 'Nobody wants you around 'ere! Do us all a favour and get lost!'

Marjorie glanced around, looking startled. 'Why don't you come out from wherever you are, and, er… well, talk to me? I have come here to listen to you.'

You had to give it to her, she was a gutsy cat. And determined. She kept going despite the insults, despite her fur soaked from the rain. She disappeared to the back of the tree to inspect the bins. One of the residents had moaned at her for twenty minutes about the waste piling up for weeks because of her cuts. They had been taking it in turns to guard their bins and deter the homeless from moving in apparently. She said she wanted to see for herself.

She slumped down amidst the rubbish, yawned widely, and stretched her legs. She dug out a remnant of fish, looked round sheepishly, and began nibbling. Douglas hung back a bit, so she didn't catch his scent.

'Aha! Look who it is, it's the evil moggy.' She froze as three sketchy toms approached her and boxed her in. 'Hungry are we, Prime Minister? Are you joining the homeless club?'

'Er, who are you? What can I do for you?' Marjorie edged backwards into the overflowing bin bags.

'Don't worry about that. We're just some downtrodden union workers. We've come to tell you that you've inflicted a lot of pain and misery on the country, and we're gonna put an end to it right now.' The burly one out of the trio pulled out a blade.

'What do you think you are doing? Just stop for a second, talk to me, that's, er… well, that's why I am here tonight. To ensure that I can help you.'

'Too late for all that, Prime Minister. You've seen all the anger and rioting, and you've continued to hurt us with your harsh policies. Thanks to you, we have been left with nothing.'

'I-I understand your struggles, I grew up on a tree estate myself, just down the way...'

Douglas took his chance. 'Back off! Drop the blade!' He jumped onto the burly one and whacked him in the face with his left paw. The blade fell onto the ground.

'Oh, look, she has reinforcements —'

'Back off!' he roared. 'Turn around and scarper!' He puffed up his tail. The hoodlums legged it. The Prime Minister was safe, thank God.

'What-What are you d-doing here, Douglas?' Marjorie was shaking. She spluttered her words.

'I'm sorry. I took the liberty of following you tonight, I wanted to keep an eye on you. It's not safe round these parts, I did try to warn you.'

'Oh my, thank you, Douglas! I don't know what would have happened to me if you hadn't shown up.'

Douglas bowed his head. 'It's no big deal, honestly. I'm just relieved you're OK. Let's get out of here.'

'Oh no. Can't miss out those branches over there, we'll get complaints. Luckily, it's stopped raining. Come on. And would you mind taking, er... some action shots of me?'

'No, Prime Minister, enough.'

'I want them for my, er, social media. Shows I'm out and about. In the community. Approachable. On their level.' Her voice trailed off.

'Please. You must be tired. Let's go home.' Douglas trudged along behind her. 'Please can we go home?' Where the hell did she get the energy from?

He suddenly heard a commotion. It sounded like some sort of rave. Or a carnival. He saw a bizarre float coming towards them. It was gaudy, decorated in bright flowers. There was a giant head of a massive black cat on the front. He prodded himself with his claws, he wasn't dreaming.

'Don't you just adore this music?' shouted a familiar voice. 'Bossa Nova, I'll have you know, the sound of the South Americans!' It was the mad Defence Secretary, high as a kite. Dressed in a garland of fresh red, yellow and blue flowers. Wonder if his donors knew he was splashing their cash on stupid customised floats. He was embarrassing himself trying to waltz.

'Hector, what on earth do you think you are doing?' snapped Marjorie. 'Turn it down, you are causing a disturbance!'

'Apologies, Prime Minister!' he shouted over the jazzy guitar. 'Thought I'd bring a little joie de vivre to this shit hole. Show this lot a good time, give them something to smile about!'

'I said turn it down! Let me be clear, this is anti-social behaviour! And why are you even here?'

'Well, I heard about the special night of canvassing, and I thought I would lend a paw! Be a team player, help you win this thing!'

'Oh, and here's Jitters! Jitters, what on earth are *you* doing here?'

'Greetings, Prime Minister. Hector i-i-invited me to a n-n-night of canvassing. I don't think I got the m-m-memo.'

Marjorie stomped off and darted up a tree.

Douglas collapsed next to a worn-out scratch wall in the play area. He was exhausted. He watched on as that fool

Hector hassled the Prime Minister and some poor resident. How the hell did he even find out about tonight?

'Hector Perp Pahpousson, Defence Secretary and key member of the government, here.'

'Hector, can't you see I am speaking to this tom?' said Marjorie, abruptly. 'Sorry about him, sir. As I was saying, I am having to, er… well, I am having to make some very difficult decisions —'

'As the nation's Defence Secretary, I am tasked with keeping you safe and secure. How do you do?'

'Hector, you reek of moonshot. Get lost!' hissed Marjorie.

'Just a moment, Prime Minister. You know, honourable sir, I have just been enjoying some Samba, some Bossa Nova to be precise. You may have heard it just now. It is good fun, you should try it some time. Vote for us, and you too will find life is one big party.'

Marjorie shoved her Defence Secretary out of the way. 'Would you like to read my manifesto, sir?'

Hector snatched a copy. 'Since when are we "Marjorie Wilson and the Freedom Cats"? Are we in your flipping band or something? Now then, sir, you may have heard some of my innovative ideas to fund our military.' He pounced about excitedly. 'And to build a beautiful, strong, border wall to keep out the immigrants, the illegals, the strays! Uh, no offence, Prime Minister.'

Marjorie bared her teeth.

'We need your vote if we are to build it,' continued Hector. 'It will keep you and your family safe.' He turned to face her. 'I say, did my border wall make the Marjorie Wilson manifesto?'

Marjorie jumped on top of her Defence Secretary. They rolled around on the branch swiping at each other. Hector slipped and clung on with his claws. The hefty tom disappeared into his cabin. Served them right, thought Douglas. *Idiots.*

On a nearby tree branch, Jitters was rolling around on his back trying to impress a middle-aged she-cat. 'Aw, hunny, you're awfully cute. Look at your beautiful grey coat. What can I do for you?'

'I'm from the F-F-Freedom Cats. The Minister for Welfare and General S-S-Sums, you may have s-s-seen my video recently on PawPad. Can we c-c-count on your v-v-vote next week?'

'I still haven't made up my mind, hunny.'

'OK, can I have a s-s-selfie for my PawPad?'

Douglas slunk off. *Shitshow.*

MANIFESTOS

Making it better: The Cats Collective Manifesto.

Foreword by Rt. Hon. Kranken,
Leader of the Opposition.

All my life I have been taught one lesson over and over again — Bad Happens. Whether it's the love of our lives that don't end up being who we thought they were, our so-called friends who let us down, our greedy bosses who put us on zero hours contracts and pay us a pittance, or those in power who turn a blind eye to poverty, corruption and inequality. Yes, Bad Happens everywhere we look. The thing is that with this government, with this ramshackle bunch of crooks, a lot of Bad Happens. But I, Kranken, promise to make it better. Whether it is life coaches for the nation, a universal basic income, or a proper minimum wage, I will make it better.

If we are to truly improve our lives, we, as a species, must evolve. We must move on past our natural individualist tendencies, and look out for each other.

Our instinctive selfish ways belong in the past. We are better off together. So kick out the crooks, and vote for the Cats Collective.

Yours truly, K.

1. We will introduce a universal basic income of 2,000 Britsh Mews so that everybody, regardless of background, breed, income, or occupation, can dream big and have the freedom to do anything they desire. (Nothing illegal of course).

2. We will introduce a compulsory national minimum wage of 30 British Mews per hour. Putting money into the pockets that really need it will mean everyone can afford to live, pay their rent, and put food in their bowls.

3. We will oppose any talk of leaving the Global Cats Alliance. Membership is good for jobs and good for trade. We can become stronger standing together, as one, with our global brothers and sisters.

4. We will reverse all planned cuts. Now is the time to invest in our public services. We will not let unnecessary scare stories of debt or false hoomanian comparisons rule us.

5. We will hire 50,000 life coaches for the nation. A healthier nation is a happier nation. (We will begin a trial of 1,000 life coaches in our first year in government, and see how it goes).

These policies will help us move on from our selfish ways. They will help us live in a fair and equal society, with poverty becoming a thing of the past. Bad Happens. But we will make it better again.

*

Back to being cats: The Manifesto of Marjorie Wilson and the Freedom Cats.

Foreword by Rt. Hon. Marjorie Wilson, Prime Minister.

I am asking for your help as we fix the economy. We tried this dangerous, hoomanistic, collectivism fad and it hurt us badly. The last government's out-of-control borrowing and spending addiction has taken us to the brink of bankruptcy. They raised your taxes and started giving it away as free money, essentially to buy your votes. Businesses went bust, and millions lost their jobs and homes. And make no mistake, if they get back in, they'll do it again. We need to remember who we are, cats. Yes, we are proudly individualistic. We want to better ourselves and provide for our families, and we shouldn't be ashamed of that.

We need to take the difficult decisions if we are to prosper once again. I grew up on the fifth branch of a tree in a rough estate, brought up by my single mother, and I know what it's like. Frankly, I am lucky I made it to university. This society pulled a moggy like me up, and in turn, the sole purpose of my government is to pull every cat up, so we can live our best lives.

We're beginning to create the jobs and we're paying off our debts simultaneously. We've come a long way in the past few months. But I must now level with you. We need to cut spending further in order to balance the books. I need to give the economy stronger medicine to make it fighting fit again. Only then can we go back to being cats, and thrive once more.

Thank you.
Prime Minister Marjorie Wilson.

1. Our welfare bill is completely out of control, we are spending billions on it. We can't afford it, and this is not cat behaviour. To remedy this, we will cap total benefits to 500 British Mews per month per family. We will not pass our debts onto our kittens.
2. We want to encourage healthy eating for everyone in society. As we cap benefits, we will introduce food stamps as part of welfare payments to discourage spending on moonshot, nip leaf and junk food.
3. We will set up a Global Cats Alliance Unit in Downing Street to immediately begin looking at the conditions of our membership. Either the Alliance reverses its overburdening regulations on

our beloved jumbo fried fish skins and nip leaf, or we leave it altogether. In either case, we will fiercely protect our borders. (Please note: we are NOT under any circumstances building a wall. We are an island.)

4. *Compulsory hunting practice will be increased to 15 minutes a day for all nursery children. We are proud of our world-class education, and it will remain free. The Freedom Cats will never introduce nursery fees.*

5. *We will double our working day from two to four hours, and scrap the right to a guaranteed 18 hours of sleep. This common-sense move will make us more productive as a country.*

6. *We will cut all taxes to a 5% flat rate so cats can keep more of their hard-earned money, and businesses can invest in our country and create jobs.*

7. *We will find one million British Mews through immediate efficiencies within government and distribute it as emergency aid to homeless cats living in the slums. They will receive this money in the first week of my new term.*

We will nurse our economy back to health with the strong medicine it needs, and show the world we are open for business. Above all, we will begin to live like cats once again.

MA

Jitters scoffed an artisan salmon and chicken biscuit, crumbs going everywhere, and he didn't care. He was elated this evening. All his carefully thought-out Emergency Money Saving Committee policies had made it into his Party's election manifesto. Even the food stamps got through. It was the slick video that did it. He was hitting the big time; the pundits were correct, he sure was one to keep an eye on.

The Prime Minister hadn't made the last Committee meeting, which was very unlike her. No explanation, nothing. Nevertheless, she was listening to him, she was taking notice. She liked him, and if they won this election (which they would), on a strong manifesto based on his sensible and costed policies, then surely, just maybe, he would become Chancellor. He could be delivering his first Budget this time next month! It didn't get any bigger than this. His ma would be so proud.

This called for a celebration. Perhaps dinner for two at the Michelin-starred *Fish In A Tie* restaurant. He started drooling at the thought of their special — roast haddock with a chorizo crust. He could murder one. Literally. Jitters took his red polka dotted necktie out of the drawer and carefully unfolded it. Tonight was a special occasion, after all.

He trotted onto the street, almost skipping with joy, and ran into a large black figure. 'Congratulations, old chap!' Ah, Hector. He was wearing a stripy waistcoat and leaning shiftily on the lamp post. 'You must be over the moon, and deservedly so. Got time for a swift one?'

'No, th-th-thanks, I c-c-can't. Got p-p-plans with my ma. Sorry.' Jitters sped up. The last thing he wanted was to get into a conversation with crazy old Hector.

'Ah, yes, your ma. A fine catess indeed, please pass on my very best, will you?'

'S-S-Sure.'

'Say, Jitters, I was very impressed with your showing in the manifesto.' Hector followed closely behind. 'You know, the two of us would be a force to be reckoned with if we put our superior minds together.'

Jitters scoffed. There was no way he would ever get involved with this... this snake. He knew about what had happened between him and Douglas. He thought of his ma again. He couldn't wait to tell her the news and see the look on her face. And tonight, they would celebrate. They would feast well. On the roast haddock special. He would also send a copy of the manifesto to Ffion in the morning. Signed with his very own paw print. Along with a dozen heart shaped biscuits. The brains behind this government's election-winning manifesto, a social media influencer, and a romantic. She had well and truly lucked out.

'Say, Jitters, old friend,' tried Hector again. 'Did you see the Global Alliance policy in the manifesto, per chance? That was down to yours truly.' He peeked over to see whether Jitters was impressed. 'Even if she wins this election, she won't last long… the cuts are hugely unpopular, I'm afraid. Plus, she is not leadership material. Now imagine a Hector and Jitters super ticket! I'd make you my Chancellor, old chap. You and I could —'

Jitters stopped in his tracks and hissed loudly. His tail puffed up. Hector froze in the middle of the road. They stared at each other intensely. It was extremely rare for him to get riled up like this. Hector crept backwards in slow motion. 'It's OK, old chap, take it easy. No drama. Just think about what I've said.'

There was no way he would have anything to do with that… that mad cat. That drunk!

Jitters approached his mansion. His mind went back to the roast haddock special, he might order two for himself. He sat outside and spent a good 15 minutes on his outdoor scratching post. It was kind of his ma to have installed it when he became a minister. It helped him when he felt anxious, almost a form of meditation. He felt the stress of his encounter with Hector slowly seep away, his claws attacking the post with all their might. When he becomes Chancellor, that buffoon had better watch out.

'Ma! Ma! You're not going to b-b-believe what happened t-t-t-today!' Jitters pounced inside. 'The Prime Minister loved my p-p-policy ideas and every s-s-single one of them made the e-e-election manifesto! I've p-p-pretty much written it, ma! And when we w-w-win the election, I w-w-will become Chancellor! Where are you, ma? I'm t-t-taking you out for dinner so get your g-g-g-glad rags on!'

Jitters was skipping around the place. He couldn't wait to see his ma's reaction. He crashed into his pile of economics books, toppling them over. Ah, there it was. *One thousand economic jokes and puns,* he'd been looking for that everywhere. He stepped on it and leapt up, athlete-like, into his elevated private room. *Jitters Renshaw's space – Keep out!* read the tatty sign. He looked into the mirror and straightened his necktie. He supped from his water bowl and straightened his heart-shaped cushion. He would bring Ffion here soon, she would like it. 'Ma? H-H-Hellooo?'

He leapt across the heights of the mansion into his relaxation corner. He sniffed around. He recognised the familiar dandelion and oat grass scents. His ma always remembered his favourite sprays. He nibbled at the grass on the wall.

'Cooo-eee, ma!' He crash landed back onto the *One thousand economic jokes and puns.* The cover promised *Guaranteed bantz to dine out on for the rest of your life.* He scrambled upstairs, knocking the framed photo of his community college graduation off the wall. He was posing next to his ma, dressed in full regalia, proudly holding up his advanced diploma in general sums. He was the youngest kitten to get it that year.

He paused and hung it back on the wall, next to the picture of them posing by a giant Patagonian Toothfish. He remembered the time they had caught it together on holiday. It was a big deal, he had just received his Level One certificate in hunting. They had definitely earnt their supper that night.

'Ma?' He scratched on her bedroom door. It felt eerily quiet and it suddenly occurred to him that none of the lights were on. 'Ma?' He walked into the bedroom and found her stretched out in a deep sleep. Well, that was not ideal. The restaurant was booked for half an hour's time. He noticed his old dusty violin at her side. *That's odd, what's she been up to with my violin?*

He crept over to her and gave her a gentle nudge with his head. She did not stir. 'Ma, wake up, you have got to get ready, I'm taking you out for dinner!' Maples lay still. Jitters noticed her body was cold. He nudged her some more and realised she wasn't breathing. His chest tightened up. He nudged her harder. She rolled over limp, without any resistance.

'Ma? Ma!' Jitter's heart started racing. His whiskers began to quiver. 'Ma, you must wake up. I have s-s-something to tell you. No...'

He trembled wildly. 'Don't leave me, m-m-ma! Not now! Please w-w-wake up!'

He realised at that point that the thing he feared the most in the whole world, the thing he most dreaded, had happened. His beloved ma, his best friend, his only friend, had left him.

'Ma. Please w-w-wake up. I n-n-need you. Your J-J-Jitsy needs you,' he howled.

He lay next to her, his head on hers, and he sobbed through the night. She was the only one who had ever looked out for him. She raised him, cared for him, and had championed him unconditionally. He could not do it without her. He would not be able to go on without his ma.

MISSING

Douglas was still shaken after the other night. They pulled a bloody blade on her. She could have died. Thank goodness he had got to her in time. And she pledged a million British Mews for the homeless in her manifesto. He didn't see that coming, and he still couldn't quite believe it. It was a small drop in the ocean, but massive progress, nevertheless.

Now it was time to fall in line, serve her as her deputy, and help her win this election in five days. And above all, it was time to prove to darling Rara that her daddy is a good guy.

He weaved in and out of the maze inside Downing Street looking for her. She had missed the monthly fish breakfast with business leaders which was unlike her. 'Has anyone seen the Prime Minister?'

'Nobody has seen her since yesterday,' said a clerk, tapping away on her computer. She looked bored.

That's odd, where the hell is she? He trotted up the grand staircase, looking at the framed pictures of previous Prime Ministers and their accomplishments. There was Augustus, teeth bared, holding a big shark-like fish. Finley and Humphrey, both decent leaders of their time, both chasing some sort of exotic looking bird. Louis, with his prince-like looks, tucking into goose. Hunting geese while in Office had been his thing. And there was Marjorie, looking nervous, wearing some sort of blingy collar. Looking down at him.

He meandered down a long corridor sniffing at the soft and luscious carpet. No sign of her.

He nosed around the Cabinet Room and sniffed out her special chair at the centre of the table. Nothing. He knew she liked to dine alone in the State Dining Room. Not today. He made his way to her study. The sofas were still there, and that horrible leather still got up his nose.

He turned on the TV. It was that lefty channel, Star News. *Why the hell does she watch this garbage?* Ophelia was being interviewed on College Green, she was babbling on about the election. Big letters scrolled at the bottom of the screen: *IS THE PM IN HIDING?*

'Let's face it, she is unpopular at home, she is unpopular with the Global Alliance, she messed up her negotiations abroad, is that why she's hiding? You only have to scroll on PawPad to read the rumours…' The Shadow Health Secretary looked high; she'd probably been on the nip leaf.

Douglas realised he was trembling. He'd last seen her yesterday, in the rough tree estate. What if she was harmed in some way? *Fuck!* Maybe this was his big chance. To get in there, captain the ship. His big chance to rescue the slum cats, to rescue the country with a calm head, and sensible policies.

He paced up and down the study and looked at the Prime Minister's family portrait. He recognised the pure white kitten sitting next to an older cat, probably her mother. He had given her so many chances to do the right thing. The trouble was that she didn't really give a toss about the needy. Besides, he had told her to be careful, she didn't listen. This was all her fault.

He thought about Rara, he pictured her gorgeous eyes looking into his, her gorgeous, disappointed eyes. But she would surely understand once he explained everything. Surely, she would see the bigger picture. Surely, she would agree that it needed to be done.

ACT THREE

ELECTION COUNTDOWN: 72 HOURS TO GO.

Douglas crept pensively to his office after his nightly river swim. He needed to find the PM somehow. Find her fast. Rescue her and put things right.

He was glad he stopped and talked things through with Rara at their special spot. As usual, she'd helped him put things in perspective. Made him see sense. Yes, Marjorie was impossible sometimes, but she was the Prime Minister. And she deserved a loyal deputy. Plus, he needed to stop showing Rara his very worst side.

The door to his office was ajar. He peered in and found a grey cat on his desk. It was the Minister for Welfare and General Sums. 'Jitters? What do you think you are doing in my office?'

A gaunt Jitters, big sunglasses covering his face, was staring at the orange fish in front of him. He batted her to and fro as it flapped and gasped for air. 'S-S-Say, Douglas, how d-d-d-do you prefer your fish? P-P-Pan fried? Grilled?'

'Oh God, Shuffles! What the hell are you doing to my Shuffles? Put her back!'

Jitters leapt onto the desk and hissed. 'What did you do to my m-m-ma?'

'I haven't done anything to your ma! Put Shuffles back! Please, Jitters, you're going to kill her!'

'Liar! I found s-s-suspicious looking packages addressed from you to my ma! D-D-Drugs!' Jitters bared his claws and prodded the fish.

'No, Jitters, just please go easy on her. You've got this all wrong. He found his moment, snatched his friend, and threw her back into her tank.

'W-W-What happened?' Jitters growled.

Douglas sighed and placed his paw on the agitated intruder. 'Jitters, I'm really sorry about your ma, and I'm sorry to say that she hadn't been well for a while. We think it was kidney disease.'

'What are you t-t-talking about?'

'Look, she got in touch with me a few weeks back. It was out of the blue —'

'N-N-No, she wouldn't have done that.'

'She did, Jitters. She asked me to pick up some medication and nip leaf for her —'

'Liar! She's never chewed a n-n-nip leaf in her life!'

'She was chewing very occasionally, Jitters. It provided her with a bit of comfort.'

'Why did she contact y-y-you, then?'

'She didn't want to disturb you, she said you were busy, going places —'

'No!' Jitters screamed. 'Never too b-b-busy for my m-m-ma! Why didn't you s-s-say something?'

'She had sworn me to secrecy,' Douglas whispered. 'She

didn't want anything to get in the way of your career, she was so proud of how well you were doing.'

Jitters started wailing.

'I was sending her medicine, Jitters. That's all.'

'Liar! I s-s-saw what you did to your s-s-so-called pal. I have been w-w-watching everything! You stabbed him in the b-b-back. I know y-y-y-your s-s-sort!'

'Listen to me, Jitters, I'm not proud of what I did to Hector. He is a bloody lunatic, though. You know very well that he is dangerous, and he needed to be stopped. But your ma, I was helping her, I know how much she loved you.'

'Kidney disease, huh? F-F-Funny that, I never saw her ever take any m-m-m-meds. Liar!'

'She didn't want you to know, Jitters, I'm sorry.' Douglas reached in his drawer and pulled out bits of crumpled paper. 'Look, here are the prescriptions I have been collecting from the vet on her behalf.'

'S-S-Something d-d-doesn't add up!'

'OK, well, I know that your father died of a moonshot overdose. That your ma saved your life when he forced you to fend for yourself as a kitten. She thought the world of you Jitters, she was proud of her little Jitsy. Think about it, how on earth would I know any of this, unless she told me?'

'B-B-But why did she contact you out of everybody?'

'She looked me up on PawPad of all places. She said she remembered me from when I came and stayed with you that time. She said she liked me. I, uh, have an honest looking face apparently. I can show you her messages if you really want to see them.'

Douglas suddenly remembered his dear Shuffles and

darted over to check on her. She was bobbing on her side inside her tank.

'No. God, no. Shuffles!' He gently scooped her out of the water. She felt flimsy. Life had left his beloved Shuffles.

'My little girl! Jitters, what did you do?'

He looked round. Jitters had disappeared.

*

The Deputy Prime Minister watched his dear friend, looking peaceful. He had washed her thoroughly with the river water, paying special attention to the cuts from Jitters' claws.

'I am so sorry I let this happen to you. Rest peacefully, my dear friend. You too will always be my little girl.'

He untied his white neckerchief and wrapped it delicately around her. 'Thank you for being my best friend. My, uh, second daughter.'

He laid her at the same spot as his Rara, before the angels had taken her away. 'You'll be in heaven shortly, with Rara. She will look after you.'

Douglas felt empty. It was time to go. The clock was ticking; he had to make things right. 'Until we meet again, Shuffles.'

ELECTION COUNTDOWN: 48 HOURS TO GO.

'Hello, anyone in?' Douglas grabbed onto the branch above, and gave it a tug. He heard something move. He scratched on the wooden cabin. 'Good morning, miss, sorry to disturb you.' He held up the official portrait of Marjorie, she had a silk scarf around her neck and was pouting awkwardly. 'You may recognise her? Uh, have you seen her?'

'Get lost.'

He'd been at it for two hours and not a single lead. Not one resident had time for him. He sniffed at the bottom of the next tree along. If she had recently been in the vicinity, he would be able to sniff her out. Especially that cheap leather smell that seemed to follow her around. Nothing.

It was time to change tack. He crept up the next couple of trees and snuck into the cabins, nosing around. Pretty much everyone was asleep at this hour.

His phone wouldn't stop vibrating. It was PawPad going crazy. He scrolled down. *The Meowington Times* had broken the news. *Fears grow for PM as she's reported missing from Downing Street.*

He found a quiet spot on an empty branch and lay down.

Shutting his eyes felt so good, he couldn't help himself. It would only be for a minute. It was all his fault, he just needed to find her safe and well, and this time he would change. He promised himself that. It was time to ditch the games and be a loyal deputy to her. He thought of Rara. And Shuffles. He would make them proud.

He heard a yelp as he started to dose off. 'Why can't somebody help me?' He shot upright and scrambled down the tree. 'Help me, please!' He sprinted towards the agonising cry. It didn't sound like her, too high pitched for Marjorie. Maybe that was the sound of raw fear.

He crept through the dense estate of trees, keeping his nose to the ground. The cry got louder. 'I am in trouble, I-I shouldn't be here. Help! Somebody help me!'

He was sure he had located the tree and hid across the way. She needed careful extraction, returning safely to Downing Street without anyone seeing. If he was fast enough, they could make out the rumours in the press were false. Fake news.

Mmf-mmf. He tried to catch her scent. He crouched down low and felt a net strangle him. 'Stop! I can't breathe!' He gasped as it squeezed on his neck.

'Stop struggling, then!' came a hoarse whisper. 'Who are you? And what are you doing here?'

Douglas felt a sharp claw dig into his neck. He squinted and made out the bright red emblem of the Claw Brigade on the collar of the aggressor.

'It's me,' he hissed. 'The Deputy bloody Prime Minister. Get the hell off me, you moron!' Why the hell had the spooks turned up? They were incompetent at the best of times.

'Look, she's up there! This will be over in five minutes. I'm going to get her.'

'No, stand back, Mr Deputy. We're trained and we're going in.' The leader of the Brigade let out a gruff meow. Nothing.

He huffed and meowed again. Still nothing.

'Come on fellas,' he pleaded in his husky voice.

Two slightly overweight cats appeared. One of them had gravy all over his face. 'Sorry, we were just fuelling up,' he said.

Douglas rolled his eyes.

'We're scaling the tree!' they declared.

'Quick strategy meeting first,' said the leader.

'We don't need a flipping strategy meeting, she's just up there!' said Douglas.

They looked up. The hysterical pleas had ended with a long whimper. The tree's residents were asleep, zonked out, blissfully unaware of the ongoing incident.

'We're scaling the tree, then,' the two spooks said again.

The three of them scrambled up with perfect silence. They dug their three-inch claws into the trunk with a vet surgeon's precision. One of them stopped halfway. 'Cat down! Cat Down!' he whined. 'My claws! They're stuck!'

'Oh, for fuck's sake,' said the leader.

Enough was enough. Douglas began climbing. The spooks sped up as they saw him catching up. The one with the stuck claws was effing and blinding. A loud squeal made everyone jump as they reached the top branch. The victim was safe, thankfully.

'What are you doing, mate? Wait, have you come to take me away? You are bad dudes!' False alarm. It was one of the estate's nip leaf addicts. 'Get off my fucking property!' she screamed. 'I don't trust you!' she added. She had lice crawling on her blonde fur. Definitely not the Prime Minister.

Douglas had forty-seven missed calls. He checked PawPad again. Rumours were circulating of a suspected kidnapping involving the Prime Minister. The news channels had picked up on it too. That explained the Claw Brigade's presence.

He spotted the three sleepy spooks napping in the play area. They were completely useless. He would finish the job himself. She couldn't be far from here. Someone in this estate would know where she was, he was sure of it. This was the last place she had been. She hadn't returned to Downing Street since the canvassing two nights ago. No scent of her anywhere, and zero cooperation from a hostile estate. It wasn't looking good.

NOW OR NEVER

Back in Whitehall, Hector was slumped in the corner of his office, fur soaked in moonshot. He stared at the breaking news story on his phone. *Fears... Fears... Prime Minister... kidnapped.* He got the gist from the blurry sentence. Was this for real? Perhaps his mind was playing tricks on him. He chewed on some nip leaf. That stuff was medicinal, especially in fuzzy moments.

He found the tatty letter and unfolded it delicately. *The decision has been made to terminate your employment for reason of misconduct.* He closed his eyes and flinched. He could see his buddy staring at him. Pleading with his large round eyes. Hector shuddered at the memory and screamed out, 'I'm sorry! I didn't mean to leave you like that, old friend!' It was too late, whatever was done was done. He couldn't turn back the clock.

He dragged himself to the cream fountain and dipped his face in it. A good gulp never failed to give him the hit he needed. The perfect hangover cure. He scanned the room, there was most definitely a rat in here somewhere, he was sure of it. So, the PM seemed to have been kidnapped, or perhaps she had done a runner. Either way, the time was ripe to make a move. His moment had come. He fumbled for his phone.

Dear Black Cat Colleagues,

It seems as if our (not so much) glorious leader may have buckled under the pressure, and done a runner hours before the election. And hopefully she has taken her bland agenda with her.

Her cowardice brings precious opportunity. We are mere hours away from a new and exciting dawn. A dawn in which we beef up our miliary, fiercely protect our sovereign land, and Make Britain Great Again!

Colleagues – have you noticed that the mentally unstable General Bulgakov has gone eerily quiet ever since the election was called? Ask yourself why. Is it because he wants our weak moggy Prime Minister to be elected back in? Is it because he doesn't want to cause any trouble for her?

My dear colleagues – it is through being bold, being provocative, and being innovative (think wall), that we must stride forward and create a happy future for our darling kittens.

I am sorry to have to remind you that neither Marjorie Wilson, nor her wretched deputy, nor the band of stuffy career politicians that surround her, are the ones to take us there. The Prime Minister, much like the ostrich that cannot fly or the short penguin stumbling around aimlessly, has zero ability to inspire or lead. If she has legged it, her equally useless deputy will automatically take her place. We mustn't ever allow that to happen. DOUGLAS SCHNITTY, FCINO, WOULD SURRENDER OUR COUNTRY!

And so, my dear colleagues, it is time to put in our letters of no confidence. I am willing and able to step up and be the leader this country is crying out for. If you lend me, Hector Perp Pahpousson, your vote, all your wildest dreams will come true. You will get value for money, and some change back! Together we will laugh, and we will hope. Together we will reach the promised land.

We must move with haste. I ask you to join me tonight in my office for a midnight moonshot tasting. I will be more than happy to listen to your policy priorities and answer any queries you may have.

Hector.

PS. Douglas, if this confidential note was to somehow get leaked to you, I challenge you to a duel! I was thinking we could hold it at our next scheduled Society meeting in a month's time. But then I asked myself, why? Why wait? I propose holding it live on national television. I have written to the producers of 'The Week in 60 Minutes' to see if we can face-off in their studios live on prime-time TV. Then everyone will get to see my prowess in war and that you are — to nobody's surprise — a snivelly little weakling.

Hector inched towards his exciting moonshot collection. He reached out for the reserve. He froze. Serious times called for serious measures. It was time to clean up. Perhaps he could have just one. He twitched sharply. 'Please, no more!' he screamed. 'Rid me of my evil temptations!'

ELECTION COUNTDOWN: 24 HOURS TO GO.

Douglas curled into a ball inside a top branch cabin. He sniffed at the warm mouse bites laid out on the kitchen table. He hadn't slept properly for two days, and his head was thumping.

'Help yourself, sweetie,' said the elderly she-cat, warming up some milk for him. He'd knocked on at least 300 cabins in the tree estate, finally someone had invited him in. She seemed very sure she had seen the Prime Minister just a few hours ago.

'Thank you for your hospitality, mam. So, was it definitely the Prime Minister that —'

'You're very welcome. I coat my mouse bites in a secret herb. I bet you can't tell what it is?'

'Uh, sorry, mam, they are indeed delicious. Going back to the Prime Minister —'

'Parsley.'

'Ah. Going back to the Prime Minister, when exactly did you —'

'I say, you are quite the looker aren't you, young tom?'

'Uh, thanks.'

'You smell divine. What's the fragrance.'

'It's a new one. It's got a hint of, uh, Tatarian honeysuckle in it, I think,' Douglas murmured.

The she-cat edged closer and sniffed his neck.

'Listen, back to the Prime Minister, please can you tell me where you saw her?'

'Well, I had just woken up from my daily kip, you see. And I had warmed up a little milk for myself. Well, I had frothed it, actually. Do you have a frother?'

'Uh, no.'

'Well, let me tell you, it is a life changing gadget.'

'Uh huh,' mumbled Douglas.

'And yes, so I had warmed up the milk first. I like it pretty hot. You'd be amazed at how hot I can actually take my milk —'

'Sorry, mam, can we stick with where you saw the Prime Minister earlier today? I really need to know.'

'Today? Oh, no. She'd knocked on the door the other night —'

'Uh, pardon, mam, sorry to interrupt, I thought you said you'd seen her a few hours ago?'

'Well, yes, technically it was a few hours ago. Quite a few hours ago. Maybe 20 or so hours ago.'

Douglas stopped himself from baring his teeth. What the hell was wrong with her?

'I told her she's got my vote,' she babbled on. 'Had to whisper it, you see, have to be careful round these parts. Can't be saying stuff like that round here.'

'Uh huh.'

'She was with her entourage, I remember you! And the

other black Chinchilla, and the handsome grey one with the cute stutter —'

'OK, but you haven't seen her today?'

'No. Why would I have seen her today?'

Douglas rose. 'I must thank you for your time, mam.' She responded with a gentle chirp. What a complete fucking waste of time that was.

*

Douglas headed back to play area to awaken the sleepy spooks. Perhaps they would have some intel, some clues, anything he may be able to go on. He noticed the trio in the distance sniffing away at the ground. They seemed to be onto something for once. He kept his eye on them. They stopped within minutes and huddled close together. Probably one of their stupid strategy meetings again. He kept back.

They were on their way again after 15 long minutes and eventually approached a patch of disused trees. He crept forward and noticed dozens of cats clambering over each other in the distance. A sharp whiff of sweat hit him. The spooks stopped and huddled together again. It looked like there were at least 50 cats from the estate fighting amongst themselves trying to get close to something.

He thought he caught Marjorie in the medley of scents. He recognised that manurey sofa smell anywhere. He couldn't be sure though, and there was no way he was getting past that crowd any time soon. He climbed up a tree nearby, heaving himself up, using all the strength he could muster in his knackered legs.

Tap-tap-tap. Tap-tap-tap. Sounded like a woodpecker busy at work. Douglas froze. The warm mouse bites had whetted his appetite, he could devour a meaty woodpecker right now. Tap-tap. Tap-tap. He had manoeuvred up the tree pretty smoothly, he thought. He looked down at the spooks, they were still nattering away in their huddle about something or the other. Jokers. Perhaps he should grow those claws. He could have a distinguished career in the Claw Brigade, rise to the top, turn the institution around. He heard the flutter of wings, the woodpecker had escaped.

There was mayhem on the next tree along. Residents crammed themselves on the wobbly branches, desperately trying to reach a cabin at the top. He caught Marjorie's scent again. Yes, it was definitely her. He caught the familiar scent of her perfume mixed in with that cheap manurey sofa leather. She was at the top of that tree, he was sure of it. He eyed up the tree, it was at least two metres away. About six times his length he reckoned. He fixated straight ahead on the target. It looked structurally unsound. He crouched onto his hind legs. Took a breath. Mustn't look down, he told himself. Mustn't think about it. He leapt for his life before he had second thoughts.

*

'I will tell them in no uncertain terms, that they must keep their, er… well, their mucky paws off our jumbo fried fish skins. And our, er, our, er, world class nip leaf.' Thank God! She was alive. Although, she sounded delirious.

The crowd started hissing.

'My turn!' shouted someone. 'How many hours of sleep have you had today, then, Prime Minister?'

'Well, none.'

'And how does it feel, you sleep snatcher?'

She was surrounded. They looked on edge, as if they were about to attack. He needed to do something before she got herself mauled. Or someone got mauled.

'Psst, over here,' Douglas whispered loudly. He was clinging onto the edge of a wobbly branch with about a dozen others. Marjorie's reddened eyes clocked him. She looked like a zombie.

'I am on the side of the strivers,' she declared.

Prrah Prrah! The sound of firecrackers and panicked shrieks made him jump. It was the Claw brigade dispersing the crowd below. The hundreds of residents and protestors scarpered. The spooks had finally come good.

Marjorie didn't bat an eyelid. 'I am on the side of the doers,' she went on.

*

'Thank you so much, Douglas. I-I owe you.'

Douglas looked down at his paws. 'Please don't say that, Prime Minister, frankly, I am just relieved I managed to find you. And that you are well.'

She looked tired and unkempt; her hair was greasy and knotted. He went over to light the fire. She had been on the derelict branch for two days. It sounded horrendous.

'What were you doing there alone, Prime Minister? I mean, we were all with you on the night. And did I not tell you it wasn't safe out in those parts?'

'I was about to leave with you all, and someone asked me if I could help them with an emergency issue.'

'Right...'

'So, I followed her up one of the trees on the far side of the estate, to a disused branch. And before I knew it, the tree was surrounded by residents and, er… well, protestors.'

'And you've been there for two days?'

'Yes, I've been busy answering their questions, trying to reason with them.'

'For two days?'

'They wouldn't let me go, Douglas. I guess I got waylaid for a few hours.'

'A few hours, Prime Minister?'

'Well, yes, technically a few. Quite a few, I suppose —'

'Look, it doesn't matter. This is all my fault; I should have looked after you better. In fact, there is something I need to tell you. I have, uh, let you down in a big way.'

'Quiet, Douglas, I won't hear of it! You rescued me, and I will never forget.'

'Yes, but —'

'You have proven yourself to be a dependable and brave deputy. I will reward you handsomely. But for now, voting is about to begin in a few hours. Let's win this thing!'

Douglas looked down at his paws. 'Yes, Prime Minister. Rest up. But you will very soon need to make an appearance on the steps of Downing Street. Let the public know you are safe and in charge. Reassure the country.'

'Yes. I will urge everyone to, er… go out and vote. I will wear my lucky pearl collar.'

'Good. There were some bizarre rumours circulating of you being kidnapped. Just deny everything, laugh it off as fake news.'

'Why, I was at home, quietly getting on with running the country.'

'Exactly.'

*

DAILY MOG
Common sense for the common cat

COMMENT: WE'RE BACKING TOP MOG MARJ

The last thing we all need is another election, but here we are. This paper has carefully scrutinised both Party manifestos, and we're getting behind Top Mog Marjorie Wilson and the Freedom Cats.

While we don't agree with some of her cuts agenda, or her nonsense sleep reforms, we admit she's got the guts to do what she thinks is right. We're in a national emergency and we need a strong leader.

We're proud that she's our first moggy, and first female Prime Minister, and we think she needs to be given longer to fix our economy and get the job done. She's right to say that since she's been in post, our debt has been falling, job vacancies have been rising, and the Siberian Cat Army have been put back in their box. However, we note that progress has been painfully slow, and there is much more to do. But at least we seem to be moving in the right direction.

The alternative is Kranken and the Cats Collective. Sadly, they seem to be in cloud cuckoo land with ideas costing trillions that would land us with the same fate as the hoomans. They seemed to have learnt nothing from history.

Let us be clear, we're only backing the Freedom Cats because of the moggy at the top. The last thing this country needs is some sort of out-of-touch, bumbling pedigree like Pahpousson or Schnitty. These foppish, posh toms do not have a clue about the struggles of the ordinary cat. They do not care about our growing slums. They are buffoons and they should never be allowed anywhere near the top job.

We think Marjorie Wilson, Top Mog, will secure a landslide victory today. If she does, let's hope she sees sense and surrounds herself with more straight-talking moggies.

Douglas emailed the comments editor.

Mam, whilst I am relieved to see you have given Marjorie your enthusiastic backing, I read your latest comments about me with intrigue. May I ask, have you, or indeed any of your colleagues, ever been forced to live in the slums? When was the last time you spoke to any

slum cats? Would you care to visit a slum with me?
Yours, Douglas Schnitty, fop, buffoon, etc.

10PM EXIT
POLL LIVE

'Maa-woooh, maa-woooh! Meeew-meeew, waaah!' Mrs Bromfield was doing her voice exercises. She lay on her side as a beautician got to work brushing her fur. Another was giving her a pedicure, trimming her claws. She'd lost weight, but best not to say anything. The lighting guy kept brightening and dimming the lights. It made Douglas dizzy.

He was in the green room inside the Millbank studios going over his lines. Yes, it was a good result, the Prime Minister was a determined character, with a strong team around her, they would now be able to get on with the job. He'd say something like that anyway. He would mention the homeless, say that helping them needed to be at the forefront of their next term. Showing empathy would be vital.

'3... 2... 1,' shouted one of the runners, 'and we are rolling!'

The audience went quiet. Mrs Bromfield walked onto the stage. She certainly had a presence about her. 'Tonight, we finally find out whether Marjorie Wilson's snap election gamble has paid off,' she boomed. Her navy blazer and gold collar looked like an outfit straight out of the Prime Minister's wardrobe.

A statistician leapt on stage and started analysing the final polls as they came in. 'Every single one is pointing to a significant Freedom Cats victory,' he said in his dull tone. 'Some have them 20 clear points ahead.'

Had to admit, the PM had made the right call in going to the country. The stats geek droned on. Wonder how much he got paid for this gig.

One of the opposition frontbenchers came on after him. Douglas had no clue who he was, he'd never seen him before. He was so boringly downbeat, he made the stats guy look like a rock god. He went on for 20 minutes, blathering on about media bias and the need for a more caring society. He eventually slunk off with his tail between his legs.

A giant countdown lit up behind Mrs Bromfield. It was 21.59 and 25 seconds. *Tick-tock, tick-tock,* almost time for the official election exit poll. Douglas sipped on the complimentary peach moonshot, courtesy of ITV. He straightened the collar of his white shirt. The tailored fit made him feel slick, it hugged his athletic body nicely. He undid his top button. He was just a regular tom after all.

'And now, the moment we've all been waiting for,' announced Mrs Bromfield.

Zoop! Zoop! Huge pictures of Marjorie and Kranken lit up, side by side, facing off with each other. Kranken looked vicious, like a stray. Had to be careful, couldn't say that in public anymore.

'The great British public have voted, the exit poll is in,

and we are predicting that… the Freedom Cats have lost their majority!'

'Oh, fuck!' Douglas gasped.

'Well, it's a shock result, that's for sure,' Mrs Bromfield continued. 'We predict the governing Freedom Cats Party have lost 17 seats, putting them on 322. And Kranken's Cats Collective have gained 34 seats, putting them on 261.'

Bromfield looked shocked too; it was bad. She fumbled around with her scripts.

'We are now likely heading for days, if not weeks of political chaos as Marjorie Wilson's Freedom Cats Party has fallen short of an overall majority. She took a chance on this snap election to increase her slim majority, and now she's lost it altogether.'

Douglas paced around. 'We've lost our majority,' he said to himself. 'Majority lost. Gone.' He heard some commotion.

'The nation has rejected austerity,' shouted the leader of the opposition, barging onto the stage. 'Do you now accept that ideological and damaging cuts lead to inequality, and do not win elections?'

Mrs Bromfield jumped towards him. 'Hang on just a minute, Kranken, I ask the questions here, not you. Now you have gained a few seats, but you still have far less than your opponents, and nowhere near enough to govern the country. Do you accept that cats do not trust you?'

'What are you talking about? We put forward a positive vision for this country, which was about bad happening, and us making it better, and we were rewarded for it in the ballot box. They liked our message.'

'It's the 50,000 life coaches for the nation that did it! Ears!' screeched Ophelia, shoving her leader out of the way.

'No, it weren't, Ophelia. Stop talking about the bleedin' life coaches, the public don't get it,' snapped Kranken. 'And I thought I told you to stay away tonight.'

A nervous looking chap poked his head into the green room. 'Mr Schnitty, you are up. Follow me, please.'

'OK, that's enough!' screamed Mrs Bromfield. 'This is live television, and I will not tolerate swearing on my programme. Now, just to be clear, you have not won the election.'

'In your opinion,' muttered Ophelia.

'Ophelia Peaches, you've won fewer seats and less of the vote share than your opponents. Some may say that technically you have lost the election. We are now joined in the studio by the Deputy Prime Minister. Welcome, Douglas Schnitty, what happened?'

'Oh, call me Doug please, and thanks for having me on your fantastic programme. Congratulations on your viewing figures, they are fantastic.'

'Thanks, what happened?'

'In fact, I read just the other day that you are officially the nation's darling. Uh, kudos to you —'

'What happened, Douglas?'

'Yes, well, look, we put forward a programme of cuts which were unpopular. Also, a little harsh for the public. But perhaps necessary.'

'It is reported that the PM wanted you to join her Emergency Money Saving Committee, she wanted your help to design the right policies to help fix the economy. Why didn't you help her, Douglas?'

'Well, I mean… the thing is… look, there are many, much better brains than mine in this field.'

'What would you have done differently if you had the top job?'

'Look, it is a tough gig, I think we urgently need to focus our efforts on helping our homeless out of the bins. Marjorie's one million British Mew emergency package is a good start. It's the biggest crisis we face —'

'Oy, weasel, get out of here! You have nothing useful to say to the country, you wretched little tom!' Hector pounced onto the set dressed in a bright yellow waistcoat. 'Hi, mam, Hector Perp Pahpousson here, Secretary of State for Defence and special friend to the… to…'

'I know who you are,' snapped Mrs Bromfield. 'Keep it civil please, I'd like to remind you that you are on live national television; the whole country can see you. Now, Secretary, was your manifesto a disaster?'

'Yahpp, of course. We've been mogged off.'

'Mogged off?'

'Yah. It was dull. There was no fresh thinking. No thinking at all. Our military is being ignored, we are being invaded by hordes of moggies from the Greek Islands, and we are nothing but slaves to the Global Alliance.'

'Don't listen to him, he is batshit,' mumbled Douglas.

'Well, sir, better a little eccentric than a limp Cats Collective shill —'

'At least I'm not a xenophobe. That too, a xenophobe who is of mixed breed himself. Hypocrite.'

'Right, that's it!' Hector thrashed his tail wildly. 'I challenge you to a duel. You and me, here and now, one on one combat on this neutral territory that is live national television. In front of the great British public!'

'Enough!' growled Mrs Bromfield, stepping in between. 'You both should be ashamed of yourselves! You are meant to be in charge of the country.'

'Hmmph,' said Hector.

'You are supposed to be role models to our kittens, what a disgrace! Get out of my studio now, the both of you!'

'You're a fruitcake, Hector,' hissed Douglas.

'I could kill you with my left paw,' mumbled the Defence Secretary, skulking off.

THE FINAL FEAST

Jitters was serving up in the Forest of the Souls. He looked up at the trees sprawled along the clifftops of Mawgan Porth. He'd chosen this special place to cook the final feast for his ma. Legend had it that the angels could get to these trees easily, meet the souls of the deceased, and fly them home, to heaven.

Deep in the forest, a barbecue-y aroma filled the air. About 30 guests dressed in black tucked into the abundance of freshly grilled fish laid out in front of them. Jitters had worked through the night preparing large chunks of grilled cod, sea bass, salmon, trout, mackerel, and giant prawns. Ma looked at peace as she took her place at the head of the table. He had brushed her fur and put her favourite emerald green necklace on her. He recognised his ma's three sisters, some nieces and cousins that he had only met once or twice before, and a group of mainly retired vets that she used to work with at the hospital.

He took solace from the beautiful dark blue sky and the waves crashing onto the rocks below. They had finished the wailing ceremony, a tradition to mourn the passing of loved ones, which had to be conducted in moonlight. It had lasted for almost an hour, guests on their hindlegs for most of it.

Jitters remembered how it worked from his religious education lessons as a kitten. The wailing was said to beckon the angels, and the louder the wailing, the quicker the angels arrived to take the soul off to heaven. The final feast was prepared for the deceased and her angel companions to enjoy before they set off on their journey.

Jitters' bones were beginning to show on his body. It had been six days since his ma had died. He had hardly eaten and had spent his days sobbing and brushing her fur.

'If... If... I can please have your a-a-attention,' he said meekly. The gathering looked on, they'd stuffed themselves for hours. He turned to his ma lying peacefully.

'Ma, I know you have to l-l-leave now a-a-and that the a-a-angels have arrived to take you to heaven. I hope you enjoyed the f-f-feast. I w-w-want to tell you that... that everything I have become t-t-today is thanks to you, your, your love... un-unconditional love and encouragement. You will always be my b-b-best friend, ma. I will m-m-miss you.'

Howls and sniffles surrounded Jitters as he walked over to his beloved ma and groomed her for the last time. 'I hope you look out for me f-f-from up there, ma,' he whispered. 'Cheers t-t-to you, ma.'

He yowled softly and felt a nudge on the back of his head.

'Ffion! W-W-What are you doing here?'

'I'm so sorry about your ma, darling. I wanted to come and pay my respects. How are you coping?'

'Well, you know, been b-b-better. It's a surprise t-t-to see you, Ffion.'

She took a step forward and gave her friend a little groom

on his neck. 'Jitters, I'm so sorry about ruining the other weekend for us. I'm sorry I went quiet. I feel terrible about what I said about your ma. I really didn't mean it.'

'I was hurt pretty b-b-bad to be honest.'

'I was just so tired, mentally drained. Work had been horrendous of late. I actually ended up quitting. I've just spent the past couple of weeks resting and recovering. No excuse, I know.'

'Y-Y-You quit? How did H-H-Hector take it?'

'He was fine, really sweet about it, actually. Shame he's so goddam crazy.'

'I often think about h-h-how we m-m-must have crossed paths all the time at work. I wonder if we w-w-would have met if it hadn't been for P-P-PawPad?'

'Funny how it all happened, isn't it? I like you, Jitters. Do you think you will be able to forgive me, baby?'

'Yes, of course. I'm p-p-pleased you came. Will you excuse me just a moment?'

*

The Minister for Welfare and General Sums crept up to the familiar face. 'Hello, D-D-Douglas.'

'I'm sorry, Jitters. I wanted to pay my respects. If there's anything I can do…'

'Th-Th-Thanks, Doug. That m-m-means a lot. I'm… I'm sorry about Shuffles.'

'It's OK, I know you didn't mean to. You smell of moonshot, Jitters, are you coping OK?'

'Not so g-g-good. You know, I was about to t-t-take her

out to dinner to celebrate and I f-f-found her lying cold and lifeless...' His voice trailed off.

'I'm so sorry, Jitters.'

'I-I-I don't know what I'm going t-t-to do without her, Doug.'

'We learn to live, and we go on. When I lost my little Rara in the river, I often thought that was it. That I couldn't go on, that it was time to give up. And I detest myself for not doing more that day. But somehow, from somewhere within you, you will muster up the strength and the will to go on.'

Douglas gave Jitters a comforting nudge and they leaned into each other. 'I'm sure she will be watching over you with pride, Jitters.'

'Any... any news from y-y-you know who?'

'Not a peep, apart from the embarrassing election night shenanigans. We well and truly took care of him. And thank you, Jitters, for all your help on the matter. Your work was ingenious. Tell me... how did you sabotage his plans so flawlessly?'

'E-E-Easy really. I f-f-fiddled with the tank, and the s-s-s-same with the plane. I d-d-drained some of the oil. As for his b-b-bonfire, I tossed a p-p-petrol can into it and that soon ended that charade.'

'Fantastic. You make an excellent spy.'

'I've seen it all now. I've b-b-been hiding in his office for so l-l-l-long, I practically live there.' Jitters chuckled.

'How did you manage that?'

'I have my c-c-contacts. He even saw me once while he was blind d-d-drunk. That's the night I f-f-found out about the article he was planning about you in *The Meowington*

T-T-Times. By the way, our scoop is being p-p-published overnight and I have even a-a-arranged delivery.'

'First class work, Jitters! I'm so pleased you spotted my recruitment ad. By the way, I have your gold watch, engraved with your pawprint, exactly as you wanted.'

'Th-Th-Thank you, Doug.'

'5,000 British Mews paid up. I will arrange delivery.'

'N-N-Nice doing business with you. By the way, there's s-s-s-something else you need t-t-to know.' Jitters looked around and leaned in. 'About H-H-Hector.'

'What about him?'

'H-H-He was behind the shenanigans the other night with the P-P-Prime Minister in the tree estate.'

'What? No way. No, I don't think that's right somehow.'

'It is. He a-a-arranged for one of the r-r-residents to t-t-trick her into the d-d-disused tree.'

'What?'

'H-H-He also arranged for all the p-p-protestors to trap her. And it was he who spread the rumours in the p-p-press about her being k-k-kidnapped.'

'No...'

'He h-h-has been t-t-tapping your phone. He can see your m-m-messages. I only recently f-f-found out myself.'

'What a lowlife. He will pay. Thank you, Jitters. You have fulfilled your contract. Uh, one more thing...'

'Y-Y-Yes?'

'Hope you don't mind me asking, but I saw you from time to time inside Downing Street, outside the PM's quarters. What were you doing there?'

'G-G-Guarding her.'

'Guarding her? From what exactly? Did she ask you to?'

'N-N-No, she had no idea. I was a volunteer.'

'What, like a volunteer guard?'

'Y-Y-Yes, exactly. I would turn up for d-d-duty three times a week.'

'But, why, Jitters?'

'Well, she was v-v-vulnerable, just like my dear m-m-ma. She needed p-p-protection from the s-s-snakes inside Westminster. Like that H-H-Hector.'

'Wow.'

'If-If-If I'd known about her canvassing p-p-plans, she would have never r-r-run into danger.'

It was getting chilly. Jitters sat alone with his ma, on guard duty for the last time. The guests had left a few hours ago and they had helped carry her to the cliff edge. He knew the angels would have taken her soul by now; he felt heavy inside. He could not quite bring himself to push her body into the sea.

WE GET WHAT WE DESERVE

Hector looked out of his office at the thousands of cardboard boxes strewn below. Whitehall was jam packed full of them. Cats from across the country were camping below, waiting to hear the news on who their new leaders would be, and what they would say.

His favourite live recital of *Carmina Burana* was thundering into the office in dramatic fashion. Fortune is indeed changeable, just like the moon, he mused. Never have truer words been belted out so eloquently. We had a chance for a landslide victory, alas the moggy blew it. He chewed some more on his soggy mint infused nip leaf. He couldn't believe the official exit poll had been spot on. The public had delivered a hung parliament for the first time in over 40 years. This election had been hers to lose. Her dull agenda flopped with the great British public. He let out a cackle. He flicked the nip leaf out of the fifth-floor window. He cackled some more.

Rumour had it that the two sides were close to an agreement over forming some sort of coalition government. If that happened, she would be out within hours. He would make sure of it. *Traitor.*

He glanced down below. He could smell the knife-edge

tension. He squinted at the various flags and placards lining the streets. He recognised the bonkers anti-nuclear lot. And there were the greens, along with the weird sharing is caring brigade. He had read that they had all joined forces to form some sort of mega crusty alliance.

Across the way, in much smaller numbers, were folk that supported the cuts, those that wanted to leave the Global Cats Alliance and members of the tax cuts lobby. They had their claws out.

Police helicopters were hovering above, and he spotted the water cannon in position on either side of Whitehall. Disorder looked likely. An announcement was imminent.

He took out his comb and began straightening his whiskers. Today was the day he had been waiting for. In life we get what we deserve, and the wretched Douglas was about to meet his fate.

Hector pounced at the scratch on the door. Who could it be? Perhaps Fee was missing him, realised she'd made a big mistake, and wanted her job back. 'Hello, hi?' He sniffed at the silver platter waiting for him. It had grilled kippers on it, what looked like a bright orange moonshot cocktail, and a rolled-up copy of *The Meowington Times*, tied in a red ribbon. 'Ooh la la, a moonshot breakfast, and a juicy exposé, served up on a platter... but who brings me this? Fee, is this your doing? Are you here? Hellooo?'

He tied his luxury white napkin around his neck and licked his lips. This was the moment he'd been waiting for. Now the whole world would find out what happened to that kitten, Rara. He supped on the moonshot concoction and spotted a note:

> *On the menu for Mr Defence Secretary this morning –*
> *breakfast kippers and moonshot cocktail. Bittersweet.*
> *(Much like my revenge.) Served up on a silver platter.*
> *Love your old friend, Douggy x*

Hector's paws started trembling. He unfolded the paper and peeked at it with a half-open eye. There it was, splashed all over the front page.

EXPOSED! DEFENCE SECRETARY DESERTED ARMY PAL AND WET HIMSELF OVER GUNFIRE

It can be revealed that Defence Secretary Hector Perp Pahpousson was kicked out of the army in shame after frequent episodes of wetting himself. His bosses decided to terminate his contract after he deserted his close friend and partner. The Meowington Times has obtained a copy of the dismissal letter, which states 'misconduct' as the reason for the sacking.

An old army pal of the Minister, who requested not to be named, told us that Mr Pahpousson used to frequently wet his bed at night. 'He used to act all tough and talk the talk. But deep down he was scared, he was homesick. He used to wet himself all the time, we all noticed it. One night, he deserted his best mate because he thought he'd heard gunfire. Well, that was the end for him. It was a shame as Hec was a good laugh and popular with the shes.'

Douglas, his colleague in government, said: 'I'm embarrassed, and a little worried, that a deserter and a coward is in charge of our nation's defences. He should do the right thing and desert his post once again. If he wets himself over a little popping, how can we expect · him to keep our country safe?'

An anonymous government source added: 'I think the whole episode really damaged him. It's why he drinks so much now, you can see he's trying to numb the memories and pain with moonshot. How absolutely tragic.'

BRAWL ON THE STEPS OF DOWNING STREET.

The media had packed out Downing Street. The eyes and claws flag was at full mast above Number 10, the bright yellow eyes flapping in the wind. Douglas lay on a nearby window ledge. Out of the way. Blending into the night. Watching. It had been a rough 48 hours for everyone. The two leaders had made a deal, it was fragile to say the least. The Prime Minister had a job on her paws to convince her backbenchers that she hadn't sold out. He had promised her he would help soften them up.

He couldn't help but chuckle at Kranken, standing awkwardly on the podium. The ginger moggy was sporting a fringe. He should have been a hooman. His ten-foot stone tablet towered behind him with the slogan: *BAD HAPPENS (But we'll make it better).*

'Does anybody know what she's doing?' Kranken called out to the pack of journalists in front of him. 'Anybody heard from her? Bloody late as usual.' He was in a foul mood, and no surprise.

Douglas had the Cats Collective HQ bugged for weeks now. Their plan now was all about getting their paws under the table at Number 10 and forcing through change from the inside. Predictable stuff, they had grossly underestimated him.

The crowds fell silent as the famous black door slowly opened. Marjorie stepped out, dressed immaculately in her pink socks and sparkly collar. She strode to her podium, avoiding eye contact with her new partner in power.

'About time,' he said in his gravelly voice. 'You're not walking down the bloody aisle, you know. It ain't like we're getting married, thank goodness.'

Douglas sniggered.

'Good evening,' began Marjorie, looking in the opposite direction. 'After many days of negotiations, detailed and intensive talks with the opposition, often painful, we have found a way to move forward and, er… well, move forward and form a national government of unity.'

She looked haggard.

'We will make sure it is for the good of our country. We will, er… redouble our efforts in creating jobs and cutting our debt. We will deliver our programme of cuts, the medicine that… that our economy so badly needs —'

'Well, we'll see about that, won't we?' interrupted Kranken.

Marjorie looked straight ahead and continued, 'I would like to thank the public for delivering my Party the most votes, but, sadly, er… well, sadly, it was not enough for me to govern alone and so —'

'Hah! You called a bleedin' election, and you lost your tiny little majority. Serves you right!'

Marjorie paused, stony faced. Douglas managed to catch her gaze. He gave a nod of reassurance. She clawed at her speech and tossed it behind her. 'Look, I entered politics to help spread opportunity and help everyone live their best lives. Sometimes those with power and responsibility need to take the, er... well, the tough decisions, the unpopular decisions.'

The hissing and booing outside the gates of Downing Street got louder.

'If we don't fix the economy,' Marjorie continued, 'we won't have any opportunities, no chances to prosper, and so this coalition government will deliver its programme of cuts, it will create the jobs, and we will live like cats again.'

Where on earth is that million she's promised the slum cats? Douglas wondered. She needs to come good in the next seven days. It's there in black and white for all to see. That policy wouldn't have existed without him. He felt proud.

'Or we will immediately throw poverty and inequality into the dustbin of history,' shouted Kranken. 'I can today tell you that we will bring in a compulsory minimum wage set at 30 British Mews. On top of that, a universal basic income for everybody regardless of —'

'No, that's not what we have agreed, Kranki, I mean Kranken. We went through the sums and everyone around the table concluded we cannot afford it. You've got to stick to the script, be honest with the public.'

'Oh, be honest with the public, huh? Be honest? Like you was back in the day when you —'

'Enough, Kranken!'

'Yes, you was very clear when you told me you loved me, then you...'

Douglas gasped in sync with the rest of Downing Street.

'Kranken, don't. Not now. We need to come together, unite in the national interest.'

'You told me that you loved me, and what happened next? I came home to our houseboat one evening, I'd hunted us rabbit for dinner —'

'Yes, fine! We were a, er… well, a thing many years back, the rumours are true, but we don't need to make the details public, Kranki —'

Fucking hell, thought Douglas.

'I'd hunted us rabbit for dinner, and I'd hidden a diamond pendant in one of its paws. It was for you. I was gonna propose to you that night, and I came home to find you at it —'

'Kranken, that is quite enough!' Marjorie glared at him.

'At it with my bloody brother!'

There was a horrible silence amongst the assembled journalists. The horrible silence spread through Whitehall.

Eugh! Douglas thought. Those two together. At it. Canoodling away. Whispering sweet nothings to each other. Eugh! His stomach churned. This was huge. The news channels and gossip columns would dine out on the fine details for months. This coalition government was already in big trouble.

Marjorie was visibly fighting the urge to wail. She was doing a good job trying to maintain her composure. Every household and every pub across the land would be tuned into this exchange and she needed to stay strong. Show her grit.

'I'm sorry, Kranki. You'll never know how sorry I am. But I must tell you, you were not easy to live with and there are two sides to every story… which I will not get into now.'

'Aha! So finally you admit that you *was* seeing my brother, behind my back!' Kranken prowled deliberately and precisely, his tail methodically swishing from left to right. 'You broke my heart. You tore it out with your claws.'

Marjorie froze; her bright white tail puffed up. 'Don't do this here,' she growled. 'Have a bit of dignity, we have urgent work to be getting on with.'

He bared his teeth and launched at her, taking a swipe with his big paw. 'You're a liar and a cheat, and you've grown into a heartless witch hurting the poor.'

They slowly circled each other. 'And I see you're still a bully these days. You've grown into a bitter old tom; your ideas are, er... illiterate. You would bankrupt the country; you'd make the very cats you say you care about even worse off.'

A frightful squeal echoed through Downing Street as Kranken pounced onto Marjorie. The new coalition partners rolled around scratching and swiping and hissing at each other. Members of the press scrambled for safety.

Kranken yelped as Marjorie's sharp teeth bit into his ear. He managed to grab hold of her and yank her into the air. She went crashing into the window of Number 11. *Shit!* Douglas ran towards her, dodging the pieces of smashed glass raining onto her. He called the ambulance.

Kranken backed away slowly, tail down, the hairs on his back spiked upright. He stumbled off past the hiding journalists, in the direction of the parliamentary medical room. Blood was dripping from his ear.

Douglas nudged Marjorie. She lay still, sprawled out on the ground. He saw a large shard lodged into her stomach.

She was losing a lot of blood. He tore off his shirt and wrapped it around her torso. Sirens and flashes of blue lights approached from the distance. The Prime Minister was taken away on a stretcher.

PM FIGHTING FOR LIFE IN HOSPITAL

By Angus, Political Correspondent,
The Meowington Times

The country is in turmoil after a planned press conference between our two political leaders erupted into a full-blown brawl on the steps of Downing Street, putting Marjorie Wilson in hospital last night.

The Prime Minister is in a critical condition and was awaiting life-saving surgery overnight to remove a large piece of glass from her abdomen. She was thrown into a window by Kranken after dramatic revelations that the two had been in a rocky relationship before entering politics. It is believed Marjorie had been cheating on her then boyfriend with his brother.

Just after 7pm last night, the two had struck a deal to form a coalition government in the interests of the country, after what has been a difficult few months politically. A source told us the week-long talks were hot tempered and fragile, with the two leaders coming close to a scrap on numerous occasions. The breakthrough came at the last minute when both sides agreed to implement an urgent programme of further cuts in return for a compulsory national minimum wage within the next three years. The Cats Collective's flagship policy of a universal basic income of 2,000 British Mews per month was the real sticking point in the testy negotiations. A spokescat for the Prime Minister said: 'Marjorie just would not entertain the conversation and quite rightly so. It doesn't matter, she should have just smiled and nodded at that mad tom. Giving away free money would never have got through Parliament anyway.'

Deputy Douglas Schnitty has now become caretaker Prime Minister while Marjorie recovers in hospital. He will now attempt to steer the country through the current chaos with Kranken as his deputy. Neither could be reached for comment.

In other government news, Defence Secretary Hector Perp Pahpousson has gone missing after this newspaper uncovered that he was thrown out of the army for deserting his best friend and wetting himself to the sound of gunfire. He was last seen on the streets of Westminster frantically waving a sword around. A witnesses said he was "off his face", looking for the Deputy Prime Minister and slurring something about a duel.

Meanwhile Jitters Renshaw, the Minister for Welfare and General Sums, the brains behind the Freedom Cats' election manifesto, and one of the Prime Minister's closest allies, has also been reported missing after the shock death of his mother Maples.

Anybody with information on the whereabouts of either the Defence Secretary or the Minister for Welfare and General Sums is urged to contact the Westminster Missing Cats Unit.

Ophelia Peaches, a rising star in the Cats Collective, said: 'What a fine mess we're in. I can confirm the leader, Kranken, is doing well. He's a little bruised this morning, but his ear has been stitched up and he looks forward to making things better for all of us. We will continue at pace with our plans to recruit 50,000 life coaches. Our country needs them now more than ever.'

*

PM IN ROMANCE SHOCKER WITH KRANKSTER

By Dave, Political Editor,
Daily Mog

Britain's Top Mog, Marjorie Wilson, is recovering in hospital after a brawl and the shock bombshell that she was in a relationship with Kranken.

A mutual friend of the pair, who asked not be named, said: 'It was doomed from the start. She used to moan all the time about his disgusting claws and meaty breath, and he used to snarl at her every time she opened her mouth.'

It's rumoured that Marjorie quickly became close to her then future brother in-law; she used to confide in him, and that closeness soon turned to intimacy. She even took him to meet her mother. One of Kranken's distant cousins, who spoke to us in return for a case of vintage moonshot, said, 'They were at it for months, soulmates turned love birds.'

In other news, we've been digging into the colourful past of Britain's new pedigree cat Prime Minister, Douglas Schnitty. We can reveal he ended up in the bins after his tot drowned on his watch, and his wife left him soon after. He racked up thousands in legal fees and lost his mansion.

We've also discovered links to a fraudster accountant and can't find any previous employment records for him. An old friend of Schnitty's informed us anonymously that he has been known to deal in nip leaf, the strong stuff that wasn't allowed under the Global Alliance regulations. We have unconfirmed reports that packages found around the Capital seemed to originate from Dodgy Doug himself.

We think you should lay off the strong stuff, Dodgy Doug, and come clean about your affairs.

MOVING IN DAY.
AGAIN

'Just a reminder, Prime Minister, that Jitters is waiting in the lobby,' said the adviser.

'Yes, tell him I won't be long,' mumbled Douglas. 'Just, uh, seeing to something urgent.'

Soft lilac cushions, *click!* Tibetan sheepskin rug, *click!* Faux reindeer hide, *click!* Blue Egyptian cotton sheets, *click!* Douglas was on the *Soft Furnishings Heaven* website. He bookmarked some curtains in Chartwell Green. And he also wanted one of those antique freestanding baths the hoomans used to love so much. That was quite enough expenditure for one day though. He rolled around in his new study, it was certainly a step up from the den. He lit the fire just because he could. He didn't care much for the thermometer telling him it was 22 degrees.

'Come in, Jitters!' he roared. 'Make yourself comfortable.'

There he was, loyal, hardworking, Jitters, thought Douglas. Kept himself close to the PM. Ended up writing pretty much the entire manifesto. He knew how to get ahead, play the game. A bit nervy, but sharp. Not one to be underestimated.

'Jitters, would you like to be my, uh, Chancellor?'

He liked his cuts a bit too much, did Jitters, but that could be worked on. The grey cat darted around the study, purring loudly.

'I take that as a yes?'

He zoomed up to Douglas, gave him a lick on the chops, and collapsed on his side.

His new chancellor listened intently as Douglas unveiled his big plan for the homeless.

'The first thing I need you to do is find 100 million British Mews urgently without any further cuts or borrowing.'

His new chancellor enthusiastically said he was on the case. He got into very precise detail about how he had already identified 65 million in savings from lower interest payments thanks to their fiscal discipline.

'Very good, Jitters.'

There was a soft scratch on the door, and in slunk four black cats in single file. Douglas felt horrible deja vu. What the hell did they want now?

'Congratulations, Douglas. We have come to let you know that every single one of the 103 MPs has rescinded their name to the no confidence letter in you. And Hector has been expelled from the Black Cats Society.'

'Oh...'

'Look, Douglas, we're sorry. We acted rashly. We got this very badly wrong.'

Crikey, those characters never apologised to anyone. Ever. 'Uh...'

'We're here to offer you any assistance you may need in your mission to help the country. Anything at all, we are at your service.'

'Uh, thanks.'

'Oh, and one more thing. The Society would like to hold a feast in honour of their new Prime Minister. Would tomorrow at 8pm suit?'

THE CONFESSION

Douglas lay next to the Prime Minister. He placed some strong nip leaf under her paw. It would help soothe her once she regained consciousness. The chief vet had informed him that the shard was successfully removed from her stomach. He had put her chances of survival at 60-40. The white hair on her belly had been shaved off; the stitches on her wound looked raw.

'Prime Minister, I don't know if you can hear me. We need to talk. Or rather, I have to make, uh, a confession.'

He was sure he saw angst in her face. 'You're here because of me, Prime Minister, and I am so sorry. I have been a horrible deputy to you. I have undermined you at every turn.'

His paws started shaking.

'Truth is, I was against your cuts. I thought they were unnecessary, uh, too extreme. I didn't help the situation at the Global Alliance meeting, I may have turned their president against you. And there's more. The scratch you got in the TV studio, even the tree estate incident, I'm ashamed to say it was all my doing.'

Douglas hunched his back and retched.

'I am so sorry, Prime Minister. I don't know what's wrong with me. I let his darkness take over, it got inside my head. I-I was frustrated.'

His voice started shaking too.

'I've let you down. And I've let down my darling Rara, and my precious Shuffles. They have been witnessing everything, watching down on me as I go about this horror movie that is my life.'

He licked the blood stain off her paw.

'I-I never meant for it to go this far. If I had been a better deputy to you, you would have won this election. You know, I have seriously considered resigning and handing the reins over to Kranken. But that would be so unfair to the country, to our kittens, and to you. He would finish off our country. Millions of dreams and aspirations would die.'

He looked away. 'So, I will do what I have to. I will fill in for you, Prime Minister. I will try my best to bring some sort of stability, and I will start delivering on your manifesto promises. And as soon as you're back, I will stand down. You will never have to see me again.'

He was sure he saw her nose twitch.

'Oh, one more thing. My first act in charge will be to begin a mass social housing programme in our tree estates. We will train our homeless to build quality cabins, and once they build them, they will get the opportunity to leave the bins and move into them for free.'

He felt that burning sensation of pride in his belly.

'We're spending, uh, 100 million British Mews to lift every homeless cat out of the slums. They will get free hunting training too should they need it.'

He slumped down and rolled on his back. He couldn't help himself.

'And we're freeing up more trees as we speak. In a few months from now, every slum in the UK will be gone.'

He was certain she twitched her nose this time. Hopefully a sign of approval.

'Oh, and, uh, in tribute to a special catess, and everything she's achieved in life, I promise to establish a gender equality and moggy rights commission. It will be named after you, and it will work to improve the life chances for millions of cats.'

He nudged her gently on her forehead. 'Get well soon, Marjorie Wilson. We're rooting for you.'

Made in the USA
Las Vegas, NV
30 November 2024

13017130R20167